After Dark

NEF HOUSE PUBLISHING

AFTER DARK

KRISTI BUCKEL

Day Eight

Beginning Again

The hell that we went through brought us together in ways I never would have imagined. What started as a day of throwing Cheetos at a fish tank ended with such sorrow that I couldn't even express it. Where we ended up was a damn sight far from where we'd begun, and the amount of loss along the way staggered me.

I missed them all. I missed the lions and their roars echoing down the hallways; the owls swooping at my head as I ran down the tunnels. My friends, both lost and found too late, and I wondered if I'd see any of them again in my next life. For most, I was sure it wouldn't be in this one. The smoke was still rising from the city center.

There had to have been something I could have

done. Some change I could have made, some symptom that I should have reported, some way I could have saved them if only I had known. Their blood was on my hands. It was on all of our hands.

But when the claws struck and the screams began, there was nothing else to do but run for our lives. Now I live in fear of everyone bump in the night. I can only wonder how soon until we will need to run again.

Run, rabbit. Run.

Day One

Evening

It occurred to me that most people's desk views did not, in fact, involve a juvenile sand tiger shark pressing his snout against the glass in front of them, coveting their precious Cheetos. I teasingly held out a crinkly orange stick, slowly waving it back and forth. Melvin the shark rubbed an unfortunate amount of nose slime against the glass—at least, I hoped that's what it was. For a second, I thought I had discovered a new form of training sharks—at least, until he ran straight into the side of the aquarium.

My name is Eleanor Rigby (yes, they were fans and no, I don't like the song)—otherwise known as Lens, more than likely due to black cat's-eye glasses since the third grade—and I may have an unhealthy addiction to punking zoo animals. (Hi, Lens!)

I let Melvin swim away, hoping he wouldn't remember this incident in another 5 minutes, but shark memory was not my chosen field of research. I sighed, swiveling back to my laptop. At this rate, my thesis, and my desire to move to South Africa, were dreams fading fast. I sighed again and started yet another email to my PhD supervisor, David, wondering what excuse I could use this time. My specialty was an extinct breed of zebra—the Quagga. But no matter how excited I was about bringing them back from the dead by the miracle of genetics and zoo breeding, I was stuck lately and couldn't figure out how to get past it. Thankfully, a doctoral candidate's best friend wandered in—a distraction, in the form of my let's-not-call-him-boyfriend, Ben. As with all good ambiguous relationships, I'd met him here at work; he was the specialist for the big cats and canids. Playing with cats that have paws the size of dinner plates had been his dream as long as re-genetically engineering an extinct zebra had been mine. We'd fallen in it's-not-love over our unique zoological obsessions.

He leaned over my discount office chair and rested his chin on my head. I watched his reflection in the shark tank glass smile, and marveled at his uncanny resemblance to Harry Potter. "What are you working on?" he said quietly, his eyes tracking the school of fish swimming by.

I cringed. "Candy Crush" was probably not the best answer. As much as my soul burned with the desire to launch myself into an African safari, procrastination had become more-or-less a personality style, rather than a personality flaw. "I'm writing to David about the Quagga project that's selectively breeding normal zebras to look like the extinct zebra, but—"

The look on his face cut me short. "Right," he said. "Hoping for an aneurysm to delete the fact that I ever asked that question. I need your opinion on something about the lions." He threw himself into the large, black bean bag normally reserved for the office cat, Hank. Hank was currently on my desk, taunting the Cheetos-trained shark with his powder coated orange fur.

"What's wrong?" It wasn't normal for Ben to ask me for advice on his kitty friends. He knew that my bent was toward prey species, not predators. I was researching the genetics and biology of herd animals; I knew about as much of what to do with his lions and tigers as I did with cooking Chinese food.

He tilted his head back, staring at the dark ceiling tiles. "Sahala's acting weird."

Sahala was Ben's favorite, the large lioness that mothered almost anything she could get her paws on. She was really bad at being a lioness, seeing as how she once let a squirrel use her for a lawn chair. Ben had bottle-fed her when he had first started at the zoo and they'd had a weird interspecies love affair ever since.

"Weird like what, because a lioness that likes belly rubs isn't exactly normal?" I spun my wheelie char around lazily, watching Ben, Hank, and the shark slowly revolve around me.

He grimaced. "I'm serious, Lens. I don't know how to explain what's wrong. It's like she's sleepwalking while stuck in a bad dream." Ben paused, staring at Hank.

Hank either had a death wish or trusted the aquarium glass enough to protect him, having stretched himself out fully, exposing his cheese powder covered body to an audience of jealous sharks.

"She's staggering when she walks, nothing like her normal prowl. Putting one foot in front of the other, which isn't the way a lion usually walks. She ran into the fence between her and the trench for patron safety three times. I mean, she's rubbed up against it to get an itch before, but it was like she was ramming it in slow motion. It's like watching an animatronic stuffed animal from those creepy pizza places for kids. She's too young to have arthritis, and I don't know what the hell else would make her joints so stiff. She keeps looking around the enclosure like she doesn't recognize it. It's just . . ." Ben's words trailed off in despair and confusion.

"Weird?" I offered to finish the thought. He nodded. Sahala was a lot like a kitten on springs, always bouncing along to the next thing she could lick. She could lovingly be called uncoordinated even at the best of times, but she still wasn't prone to walking into walls. "Has she ever done that before? Acted out-of-the ordinary? Maybe it's breeding season come early ."

"No," he said, putting his head in his hands. "Never. I just wanted a second opinion before I called the vet."

I knew that Ben was afraid to call the vet. Zoo lions could live to almost 20 years old—maybe longer, if they were babied like Sahala—but somehow, we always compared them to regular cats, including the tendency to fuss over them and think every health problem might be fatal. She was only eight years old, but that didn't make the thought of something being seriously wrong any easier for Ben. I sighed on behalf of my not-a-zebra as I committed myself to one more thing that was not my PhD. "All right, I'll go with you."

Ben and I didn't talk much as we walked through the access tunnels behind the exhibits. The zoo stretched around us in an oval, with the aquarium and research center on the "top" and the front gate on the "bottom." The paths were ringed, so that employees and patrons alike had to go through either our Super Secret Research Center, or the aquarium tunnel to finish their tour of the zoo. The "hidden habitats" were on the inside with the tunnels. Cold weather, needing treatment, bears in bad moods—they all had a place to hide from the teeming masses of screaming children.

As we walked past the zebras, I sighed again, briefly watching the herd graze through the tiny viewing window. It calmed me to look at them; I could see the patrons through the one-way glass, and it made me shudder. I can't remember how old I was when I discovered that crowds send me into a rage-filled panic. Setting the birthday present table on fire at my sixth birthday while hiding under it should have been a big clue. It's not accidental that my dream job was sitting in an open field surrounded by animals rather than people. Either way, Ben was like me and always took the less peopled route.

By the time we reached Sahala's neighbors, our gay jaguars, the lack of noise from the lion habitat whispered of how serious the problem was. Sahala was a sweet cat who loved on squirrels, but she was personally offended by pigeons. The winged rats taunted her with the same carelessness that Hank played with the shark. Sahala typically spent most of her time leaping from rock to rock, growling at the tiny flying food that she could never quite reach. This endless feline-pigeon warfare made a tremendous racket on a normal day. But there were no sounds of a jumpy, bird-chasing lioness today or the fluttering wings of a pigeon's narrow escape.

Sahala had retreated to the corner of the habitat, wedging herself between the big rock cave and the cat hammock woven together from fire hoses. Ben let us into the private habitat in the tunnel—usually a cue to Sahala and her mate Luka that a special treat had arrived, and it was time to get their behinds into the habitat. Neither started towards us.

Luka was crouching by the lions' pond, ears flattened like a startled kitten. He lay low in the grass, eyes trained on Sahala, but this was no game of tag. He was barely breathing, trying to make sure his mate didn't see him as he hid. Tiny chuffs of unhappiness withered on his jowls. I frowned. Luka usually followed Sahala around like she was his seeing-eye-lion; the fact that he was hiding from her was scary. I scanned the area, leaning up against the door to see through the glass, before falling back on my heels. "What the hell is going on?" I whispered to Ben.

I overturned a spare water bucket and climbed up for a better view. Sometimes it was hard to remember that Sahala and Luka weren't house cats; they loved to goof off and acted pretty much like Hank on a usual day. This, however, was one of those moments that called on every caveman instinct at the back of my brain to run: when I looked into Sahala's eyes, I realized that no one was home. She wasn't there, the lightness in her eyes that I normally associated with psychotic good cheer had been turned to flat dull dust. I turned to Ben, trying to speak quietly. Some part of me didn't want to let Sahala know I was there. "A fever maybe? Can lions get meningitis? And maybe Luka smells it or something?" I paused, the urgency thrumming through my veins. "But I've never seen a fever make something act like that."

"I'm pretty sure they can, but I've never heard of it happening. And where would she get it from? Isn't it, like, fluid-contact contagious? I seem to remember the health office harassing me as an undergrad to get a vaccine so I didn't get sick off someone's contaminated Coke can." He paused, running his fingers through his hair. "I think you might be on the right track, but what's making Luka look so terrified?"

It was usually Luka's job to entertain the guests during the day while Sahala protected them both from the pigeons, but at night, he was all love machine. He was a full-grown adult lion, weighing more than 500 pounds. While it wasn't unusual for him to sulk after losing a lover's spat with Sahala, the way his ears were pinned back, and the way the whites of his eyes were showing told me that whatever this was, it was not a normal fight. "I don't know," I whispered softly. "Unless he just doesn't want to get sick."

I paused. "Have you been in there?" It wasn't a question I asked lightly. Ben trusted them—but he trusted them to be wild animals. He trusted that if he did something stupid he'd get eaten, and that if he respected them and their rules, everyone would end up purring. This attitude was a world apart from mine where I generally assumed that anything that big that also ran faster than me would consider me meals-on-wheels. Ben was considerably braver. I couldn't imagine him being afraid of Sahala and Luka. But I almost hoped he was afraid of them today.

As we stood staring at the window, Luka attempted to crawl behind the rocks to their waterfall for a drink. Ben relaxed and turned toward me, right before it all went from bad to worse.

Out of the corner of my eye I saw movement from Sahala. My skin began to crawl before my eyes met hers. She walked woodenly, as if her knees refused to bend. There was no sleek stalking, no indication of her huntress nature, as she made her way toward the waterfall and their river. It was somehow all the more chilling to see her stumbling through the grass. Her amber eyes had grown so very dull, and she stared straight ahead toward Luka.

It felt so much like a train wreck. Luka was quaking, backing away from the water. I knew I couldn't react in time to change whatever the outcome was, but I also couldn't look away. It reminded me of why I'd chosen prey animals instead of predators: because deep down, I *felt* like a prey animal, and it was almost as if Sahala knew it. Sahala's head flew up, the quickest movement she'd made since we'd watched her—and she scented the air. Luka stood warily on the other side of the river that divided the habitat, using it as a defensive moat.

One giant paw stepped forward, then another, as if Sahala had forgotten how to walk. Luka lowered himself onto his belly, crawling backward. The ground shook with the power of his low growl. I waited helplessly for the sound of thick claws hitting flesh.

The sound Sahala made was inhuman. *Well, of course it was*, I thought numbly. She's a lion, not a human. But no lion had ever let loose such a sound. Her roar sounded as if she were gargling marbles in a blender. Luka looked terrified, backing himself into the rock wall. He'd put as much distance between them as possible.

I rushed to open the cage, to let him in the back habitat, but Ben pulled on my arm. "Look."

Sahala had stopped at the stream. She stood achingly still, staring at the water as if she wondered what it was. A shrill, keening wail filled the air; it sang from her slackened, open mouth and echoed against the rocks. She acted to move forward, and stopped again at the water's edge, hissing in frustration.

"She won't cross the water," I whispered. "What the hell is going on? She loves to swim."

Ben straightened and adjusted his glasses. "I don't know," he admitted as he searched for the habitat keys to shift the animals into the back habitats. "But I'm pulling Luka out of there while I still can."

"I'll call the vet," I said, but Ben was already gone.

#

The birds were gone.

Not merely silent, but gone. As I walked toward the offices and Ben took off to take care of Luka, it took me longer than it should have to notice the quiet. Birds flew in and out of the tunnels all day long, begging for scraps of food and generally enjoying being pains in the ass. I was convinced that there was an owl's nest full of fugitives hidden behind their exhibit, bent on taunting the owls not smart enough to escape. It was a background of cacophony, something I never really noticed until it was gone.

I didn't see any swooping sparrows, or the odd cardinal brightening the concrete. As I made my way back, I tried to spy through the tunnel windows out at the animals. Before I hit the owl's enclosure, one of the other big cats' enclosures was on the way. I would never be sure why I did it, but I went toward the jaguars' viewing area. A single pane of glass, no matter how thick, never felt quite as adequate as I wanted it to when I looked at the predatory animals. The birds remained silent. I couldn't hear Lenny and Carl chuffing at each other, nor could I see them up in their favorite tree. My heart dropped as I saw them, facing the wall between their habitat and Sahala's . . . staring as if they could see Luka cowering through the fake stone.

Their bright, copper eyes looked dim, but thankfully didn't mimic the death in Sahala's eyes. They were still moving, almost pacing in place, showing more coordination than Sahala had. I watched their enormous feet claw at the ground and it suddenly occurred to me that I wasn't sure if zoo enclosures for big cats had concrete buried under the dirt to keep the cats from digging under.

I wanted to run and find Ben. Hell, I wanted to run for the zebras and hide in the savannah. The jaguars weren't acting the same as Sahala, but something was clearly wrong. It suddenly occurred to me, however, how stupid it would be to go look for him. What was I going to do, pull a shotgun out of my ass and rescue him from the lions? As much as I was mostly a herd-species zoo vet intern, geneticists-in-training didn't usually have a concealed carry. Now that I thought about it, I wasn't sure you could conceal carry a shotgun, anyway.

I paused, halfway to the aquarium and the offices. Apparently, my body had made its own decision in lieu of my brain. It occurred to me that if veterinary medicine was going to end up so violent, I might just need to suck it up and go crawling back to the gun class I'd gotten kicked out of. (Instructors didn't think it was funny when your answer to "Why are you here?" involves the zombie apocalypse.)

No one was in the aquarium as I passed through on my way to the research center. I had to admit relief; explaining why I had lion shit on my socks and looked far more worried than that particular situation called for didn't seem like something I could muster enough patience for.

I threw myself into Hank's beanbag and stared at the staff's side of the big aquarium. I'd informally named all of its inhabitants as I pretended to work on my thesis, and I watched Magnus the sea turtle swim slowly toward the piece of coral that he'd designated as his girlfriend (or boyfriend, I didn't judge. Gay jaguars and all.). Something was clearly not right in Zooland. I'd never had a cat, present pissed-off Hank excluded, but I knew that generally it was a bad sign for one to face off and growl at the other. Jaguars generally also shouldn't be trying to burn a hole through concrete with their eyes. I suddenly wished I'd spent more time on zoological diseases; or at least that I'd spread around my education past prey animals. Or, on second thought, that I hadn't left Ben alone with the lions.

Even my concern about Ben didn't generate enough stupidity for me to go looking for him, however. As I settled in to wait, I started looking up symptoms on my phone while simultaneously trying to find the vet's number in our ancient Rolodex. I was always vaguely surprised that they still made Rolodexes. Rolodexii? At least soon we'd have someone with a clue of what the hell was going on.

Day Two

Way Too Early

The vet was scheduled to come at six a.m. I sat in one of Ben's oversized shirts on my favorite squishy armchair at his apartment, watching the clock more than the news on TV. I'd crashed at his place after I'd gotten home a few hours prior, not wanting to make the trek to my apartment across town. Besides, my not-a-boyfriend had a better place than I did.

The more that I thought about the events of the previous day, the weirder it got. I was pretty sure meningitis didn't make you want to attack your friends. I'd definitely not heard of a meningitis outbreak at a zoo—at least, for as long as I'd been in the program—and I was beginning to think the worst. I definitely remembered a vaccine lecture about meningitis and brain damage in college. If that's what this was, we were in trouble. It kept getting more and more surreal the longer I considered the outcome. We could lose entire habitats; hell, we could lose entire species of animals with a situation like this.

I held my Pekoe Black tea in my favorite cup: a rhino, its tail the handle. Ben always made fun of me for playing with the tail; I had a nervous habit of running my fingers up and down it, which apparently looked suspiciously like stroking a rhino's butt. Tail in hand and unmolested, I turned to get up and abuse the toaster when the news caught my eye.

□□ Headline News □ New Flu Strain Sweeping the Nation □ Citizens should take sanitary Precautions □ Vaccine in Trial Stages □□

Ben stumbled in, fresh from the shower and still lacking in that "awake" thing; he could fall asleep a lot more easily than I could, and had gotten a few hours after we'd gotten back from the zoo. He usually worked the evening shift, taking care of his cats for the night, tucking them in or whatever it was that he did. It was unusual to see him up before noon; we only saw each other at the end of my shift at work, and between us both at one of our apartments. It made the vet situation even more worrisome; if he was willing to get up this early for his cats, what did he expect to happen at the appointment?

He unceremoniously dumped a plate of cold pizza on my lap and fell sideways onto the ottoman with his own. "Kill me now," he moaned.

I poked him with my toe. "If you get this flu thing I might not have to."

"What flu thing?"

I gestured to the TV with the aforementioned toe. "The flu-pocalypse that's terrorizing babies, the elderly, and the infirm, just like every other damned influenza virus has since the dawn of time." I shook my head. "They over-sensationalize everything. This is the first time I've ever heard of it being bad enough that they made a second stab—haha, get it, stab?—at a vaccine mid-season, though. Usually they just go for the predicted strains and hope for the best."

Ben frowned, halfway through his second slice of pepperoni and mushroom. Heathen. "I've never heard of that either," he said. "And I think I took more medical classes than you did."

I stuck my tongue out at him and shrugged. "Good thing we work with animals, then, not people. You couldn't pay me to have that many people coughing on me. Come on. Some of us have meetings and actual work to do today."

His expression darkened. "I wish that was all today was going to be."

I reached out and touched my fingertips to his greasy palm. "Sorry. I know you're worried about her." As much as I made fun of Ben and His Big Cats, I knew he loved them fiercely. Watching something go from a bottle-fed runt to a powerful animal capable of taking down my poor African not-a-zebra did something to your heart.

He got up and shuffled through the clean clothes basket that was permanently stationed on a fish tank stand. "I just can't shake the feeling that this wasn't just a weird day for her or a fluke illness," he said. "Something is really wrong, Lens."

"Then Dr. Warner will help us figure out how to deal with it. We'll figure it out." I paused, taking a bite of my blissfully mushroom-free pizza. "I have to go see David today after we're done with the vet. He has a Master's in virology; maybe he'll know something about animal meningitis."

Ben pulled a fresh shirt over his head and closed his eyes. "As long as someone figures it out," he said. "I don't think I've ever seen one of the cats—or the canids, for that matter—act like this before. I don't think I've seen *anything* act like this before."

I stretched and stood up, turning off the TV. I had enough bad news coming; hearing how the new flu in the South had started creeping toward the Northeast and New England wasn't helping. With any luck, both the flu and Sahala's illness would die down quickly.

#

The thing about exotic animal vets is that they normally don't have regular office hours. Or offices. I was used to being out at the zoo for four a.m., but judging on the five o'clock shadow on Dr. Warner, he'd had a late night.

It was safer to assess the lions when the sun came up—while they weren't truly nocturnal, no cat, big or otherwise, could resist napping in a good patch of sunlight. It was o'dark hundred, however, as I peered into the habitat and saw Luka laying on his side, panting heavily.

My attention was split between him and the view behind him—Ben trying to keep Sahala back with a catch pole in front of her indoor habitat, and Dr. Warner with a tranquilizer gun at the ready. This was not looking like a good day. Sahala was stumbling—I guessed that Dr. Warner had already gotten her with the darts—but she was lunging forward, pushing against the pole instead of trying to get away.

I hesitated, knowing I'd hinder more than I'd help. I was out of my depth here. I walked over to the double-caged winter enclosure and peered down at Luka.

If a lion could sweat, he'd have been swimming. Luka lay unmoving except for the heaving breaths that escaped him. I could see the whites of his eyes, large and afraid. I'd never wanted to comfort a lion before just then.

I heard exclamations in front of me. Sahala was caught in the pole, pushing hard against it, toward the men trying to guide her. Ben staggered back slowly, toward the back wall of the tunnel, and I saw five darts in her hide as they directed her through the pathway.

Five of Dr. Warner's special darts would take down approximately one and a half elephants. Sahala should have been on the floor like a flat lioness pancake with all of the tranquilizers in her system, yet she was still standing—not only standing, but moving.

I hauled the outside habitat chute shut and went to the safety gate that would protect us from her as Ben and Dr. Warner slowly led her inside the winter habitat. It was hard to tell if the sedatives had taken effect; she was stumbling, but she had been yesterday, anyway. As Ben and Dr. Warner shut the gate, I watched as Sahala stood, a slow, groaning growl escaping through her lips with every breath.

She unsteadily set one paw in front of the other, her heavy treads echoing in the concrete room. There was a small hallway between her and Luka—lover's spats and all—and she marched toward Luka's side, one step at a time, until she reached the industrial chain-link that gave us access to her for shots and training.

Ben and Dr. Warner had gone around to the side to come into the tunnel, and I'd never been happier to see a veterinarian carrying a gun. Sahala walked on until she touched the fence, pressing her nose hard into the chainlink. It strained against the force of her will, the metal groaning in protest as she threw her whole body into the motion.

"What is she doing?" I whispered, pacing between enclosures.

Dr. Warner was trying in vain to find the right key to open the door. I didn't know what the hell he thought he was going to do once he got in there. I watched his hands shake; it was something I'd never seen before, no matter what he'd faced, what animal or problem was in front of him, he was the steadiest man I knew. But it was as if Sahala didn't know—or couldn't feel—that the fence was there, that the wire was pressing into her face—and none of us knew what to do to stop her as she walked forward.

My hands hung limply at my sides. It wasn't just a horrible situation; I also knew that I would never get there in time, that it would be more dangerous for me to help her than to let her do this. All I was there for was helping Ben and Dr. Warner shut gates; this was not my circus. I heard a soft keening noise, and it took a long time to realize it was me.

Sahala continued to walk forward, relentlessly. Beads of blood sprang up on her muzzle, staining her beautiful fur. I could hear Ben screaming as red lines appeared across her face, hear Dr. Warner banging against the gates, but I could only watch as she strained with a strength I didn't know she had to get to Luka.

Her muzzle began to fall away like Parmesan in the grater. Her dead eyes never left Luka's. He was cowering, shaking violently at the back of his enclosure, buried underneath a soft bed of straw. She pushed, hitting the bones in her nose, her face, teeth chipping and flying away. I dimly felt a fang embed itself in the side of my hand.

I hadn't seen Ben leave, but I saw him come back. A not-widely-known fact is that there are usually at least one or two real rifles at the zoo—it's a job casualty of dealing with thousand pound animals that think of humans as food. Our eyes met briefly. He closed his for a single moment before he took the shot.

Fun fact: a lion's brain is the same color as ours.

Luka hadn't moved.

The sound of Luka's breathing mingled with the ringing in my ears. I stared at Ben as he rocked back and forth on the balls of his heels. Dr. Warner tried to clear his throat. "What in the hell just happened?"

I stared at Sahala's still-warm body, looking at the chipped ruins of her teeth, and glanced over at the death grip that Ben had on the rifle. "She had her own Facebook," I muttered. "The patrons are gonna be so pissed."

Inappropriate, party of one.

Day Two

A More Reasonable Hour

It had taken a long time to coax Ben out of the employee showers. "It's still on me," he whispered, over and over again. I took the pumice stone—definitely not meant for scrubbing—away from him and helped him to get dressed in the scrubs he left at work, just in case. I somehow didn't think this contingency plan involved a lion going 'squish.' I had no idea how the zoo was going to handle this. Would I be in trouble for even being involved? I was just an intern. And the look on Ben's face screamed "damage" that I knew I couldn't fix.

Dr. Warner was waiting in the office after we took the long walk through empty tunnels. The rest of the zoo staff were avoiding us; it was clear that something happened, but management had seen the vet's truck and assumed it was a slightly abnormal euthanasia gone wrong. No one had guessed a lion would go kamikaze.

The vet was currently wearing a path in the gray carpet in front of the aquarium wall, closely followed by Hank the cat. Hank was always game to annoy humans, especially by being the world's best cat mimic. He even had his Serious Cat Face on.

"Your cat just killed itself," Dr. Warner said, running his fingers through his thinning hair. I felt bad; he was still in his thirties. I wondered if we were doing it to him.

"No, she tried to walk through industrial wire as if it wasn't there," Ben corrected numbly. He sat down in Hank's bean bag chair, burying his fingers in orange fur—thankfully not the same color as Sahala's—after Hank dove into his lap. "I don't think she was trying to kill herself. Not on purpose." He shook his head, scrunching his fingers deeply into Hank's fur until he meowed questioningly. Ben rested his forehead on Hank's, closing his eyes. "It was . . . it was more than that. She was driven to it. There was something in her that drove her to do this."

I spun slowly in my office chair, listing slightly to the left. I really needed to steal someone else's chair. Maybe Fran from accounting. As I watched the sea turtles lazily glide above me, I sighed. "That's the thing. She acted like she couldn't feel it. What would drive an animal to ignore pain like that?"

Dr. Warner scrubbed at his face with his fingers. "I've never seen anything like this," he admitted. "I thought you'd called me out here for meningitis, like Ben suggested. It's rare, but it's not outside the realm of possibility, if you'd gotten new animal shipments lately. But unless this is some strain I'd never heard of, I have no idea what the hell this is," he said. He sat down on the floor with his back to the tank, resting his head on the cool glass. I felt bad for him; Dr. Warner was who we went to for answers, and there were no answers to be given.

"Can animals get psychosis?" I tapped my pen against my desk, staring at the sea turtles. I'd never before wished that I studied disease instead of genetics. This must be how the CDC felt every time flu season came around—everyone had ideas, no one had any idea.

"Yes, but I've never seen anything like this," he persisted. "They generally attack, not . . . walk through walls. She would have gone after the fence, trying to tear it down. She would have seen it as an obstacle, not . . . acting like it wasn't there at all. I don't know *what* this is."

"Isn't that sort of what happened, just . . . escalated?" I asked. "She wanted to get at Luka—she still wanted to attack him. She just didn't register that the fence was there. So maybe it's just a different type of psychosis, one where she's just so desperate that obstacles don't matter." I knew this was slightly out of my area, but I'd taken enough elective virology classes that I could hold my own in the conversation.

Ben hesitated, fingers buried deep in Hank's fur. Hank, for his part, looked both deeply pleased and eminently disturbed. "I'd say you're right, except *she didn't care it was there,*" he said. "Animals aren't stupid, even when they're sick. It's weird that she didn't tear it down."

"Whatever this is, causes lethargy, something like sleepwalking and arthritis, and single-minded aggression, then," I said quietly. "I don't think we know what we're dealing with here."

"And a complete resistance to pain," Dr. Warner added. He shook his head. "I need to perform a necropsy on her," he said as he walked toward the door. "This isn't meningitis. I want to find a diagnosis before it's too late for Luka. Come help me load her up, Ben."

I offered Ben a sympathetic look as he went off to handle the body of a dear friend. I looked around for Hank, finding him taunting the shark I'd been . . . "training" yesterday. "Too bad I think it's already too late for Luka," I told Hank. I found myself choking on my words. As much as I liked sardonic humor, seeing Sahala try to kill herself to get to Luka . . . it hurt. It hurt to know that one of Ben's kitties was not okay, and God, it was painful to see.

Looking down at my hand, I slowly picked at a piece of tooth that I was holding tightly in my hand, numbly rooting around in my desk drawer for a little baggie. Maybe Ben would want it as a souvenir.

I turned back to my not-zebra Quaggas, my thesis, the culmination of five years of work, determined to make progress on *something*, if not what I really wanted to be working on. Maybe genetics really would have the answer—to something, at least.

#

Jeff—the lead geneticist that took care of animal breeding and the outreach coordinator for programs like mine at the zoo—met me and half of the animal care staff and management in the research center. We always had "come to Jesus" meetings there; the big boys felt that the aquarium kept people from getting quite as angry about budget cuts. Personally, I felt like this meeting was a bust from the start—if Jesus had ever hung out at our zoo, he certainly had punched his ticket out this morning.

"We had a regrettable incident occur in the lion

habitat this morning." The overseer, manager, owner—useless lump, whatever you want to call him—stood with a ray swimming over his head behind him, like a demented halo. He was the only one in the entirety of the zoo who wore a suit. It very clearly showed the divisiveness of the staff—which of us actually cared for, and cared FOR, the animals, and who didn't.

He cleared his throat. "Due to a suspected neurological problem, Sahala, our lioness, had to be humanely euthanized by Dr. Warner this morning." It wouldn't do to say 'A keeper had to shoot a lion while the vet stood by trying not to get eaten.'

"Bullshit," coughed every one of us that had heard the gunshot. Humanely euthanize, my ass. Kill or be killed, maybe.

"Dr. Warner is performing a necropsy to discover the cause of this incident. In the meantime, let's not panic. Business as usual. We'll open on time and the lion exhibit will be blocked for maintenance. Make sure to have your best smile on for the patrons!"

Business as usual. When a lion filleted herself. Right.

Those of us in the mix of research and/or specialty animal care looked around and came to a decision. We would save Luka—rumors traveled fast—and figure this out. We had to.

I looked at Jeff across the room, knowing that we wouldn't have time to talk, and tried to psychically contact him. I knew that Jeff dealt with breeding, but he might have seen birth defects or illnesses that mimicked what was wrong with Sahala. I sighed and turned away, picking up my thesis binder and pausing to look back at the aquarium.

It was always so peaceful. None of the animals fought each other (not seriously, anyway); everyone just swam their hearts out and minded their own business. If only we could all do the same.

#

Traffic to the college looked like a funeral procession in overdrive. Everyone was driving with urgent slowness up Interstate 91 in a vaguely Canadian direction. My little private college—the one with the really nice scholarships from rich, dead New Englanders—appeared painfully, inch by inch, behind a rather nice red brick wall covered in moss and vines. Driving through the low archway always made me feel like I was going on an adventure to a secret castle.

I really needed a sword.

I pulled around to the greenhouse parking behind the science building and wandered up the small, winding staircase. I was told the original building was built by an Irishman, who officially gave less than two shits about New England winters. The college was still trying to figure out how to put windows in arrow-slits without destroying the original architecture.

The second door to the right housed the virology and genetic biology suites. I guess I understood why the two went together, but it creeped me out that my department's genetic research could fuel more viral vectors, designer viruses, and general Really Bad Things, if it would fall into the wrong doctoral hands.

Dr. David Barnes was staring intently at a microscope when I walked in. "Are you expecting it to stand up and dance?" I asked, dropping my two-inches-thick research binder onto the lab bench. Needless to say, I was a little obsessed with Africa. My research wandered far and abroad of the Quaggas and the Quagga project, and I was unashamedly unapologetic about it. The thought that so little climbed out of the primordial ooze and became so much more gave me hope that eventually, mankind would get its shit together.

Not that I'd hold my breath or anything.

It was always amusing to watch a grown man almost fall off his stool. "Lens. Sorry, I completely forgot about our meeting. The CDC . . ." David shook his head. "Anyway. How's the work coming?"

I sat down on the hard, green chair across from him and slid my binder over the black table. "What about the CDC? Are you looking into that flu thing? And I'm working on how we genetically modify extinct animals. We give them so much that they didn't have—antibiotics, genetically modified food, modified DNA in the petri dish—I think we're going to hit an extinction wall."

He finally pulled away from the microscope and inexpertly dodged my question about the CDC. "Explain."

"The Quagga project," I said. "They're selectively breeding and genetically modifying embryos. But they're breeding for external appearance, not for behavior or intellect. The pseudo-Quaggas will *look* like what evidence shows Quagga looked like, but they won't be driven behaviorally by the same genetic code, they won't work in a herd the way genetics prodded Quagga to do . . ."

"So what you're saying is that in the end, we're creating lookalikes without the same genetically dictated behavior, and we're going to hit the wall where we can no longer work toward eradicating extinction in an animal when we no longer have appropriate DNA to analyze."

"I also doubt Quagga ate genetically modified plants," I added helpfully. Don't get me wrong, I'm not against genetic modifications. My entire thesis depended on it. What I was against was the thought that you could breed pretty animals and expect them to behave like something they've never been.

David frowned. "That's true," he offered, stretching slowly, hands behind his back. He shook his head, thick black glasses falling down his nose. As I waited for him to think, I watched him carefully. His brown hair was crimped and curled from lack of combing; his blue eyes were bloodshot.

I hadn't noticed the radio playing softly in the background until it squawked loudly, mimicking the air raid sirens that still went off accidentally every few months or so. It was a great way to spill coffee on yourself. While it probably wasn't good etiquette to shush your Phd mentor, I held up a hand and leaned in.

". . . CDC advises caution. The strength of this strain means that populations not previously included on the danger list, such as the elderly, the infirm and infants, but also able-bodied men and women are at risk as well."

"This is an awful lot of press for influenza, isn't it?" I asked quietly.

David hesitated, and that moment of silence

made my stomach grow cold. If anyone could read between the lines, it was David. "I don't think it's the flu," he said finally.

"Then what is it?"

He shook his head. "I don't know, but I've been a virologist long enough to know that we're not being told something important. I think it's going to become a pandemic, and the CDC and WHO are afraid of what billions of paranoid people would do in order to stay safe."

I paused, considering this. Before he fell sideways into the world of viral genetics (and fell in love with Africa as much as I had—it was why I picked him as my mentor), David had been one of the people that places like the CDC called when there was a measles outbreak. He'd hung up his proverbial virology hat for specializing in the genetics of viruses and how they grow and change—but he was still the best person I knew to look at a living virus and find out which links were missing.

David was beginning to have the pallor of a man who was living on coffee and Twizzlers. As I sat and listened to the radio, he put his head in his hands and sighed.

"I'm sure I'm over-thinking this. They're sending me a sample of the virus that's going around for me to look at. I've got last years' flu virus here, and I'll see what I can do. Stop procrastinating—how's the job at the zoo helping with your thesis?"

That, I actually had an answer for. "I've been observing the behaviors of the herd animals to see what similarities I can find, and the differences I've noticed are supporting my theory that . . ."

The problem with doing what you're supposed to be doing is that distractions provide opportunities to talk about something else. If you stay on topic, you might never ask the viral specialist if there's something out there that can make an animal turn a fence into a cheese grater for their face. And you may forget that the jaguars next door were acting a little squirrelly, too. You may forget it all as you get wrapped up in things that feel more important, and the trauma of the day would stay a tiny, niggling seed that tickles the back of your brain, an opportunity lost, and you'll never know what might have been.

Day Two

Really Friggin' Late

I sat at our favorite booth at Marzollo's, the pizzeria down the street from Ben's apartment. We were rarely at my place—Ben lived in a funky college neighborhood with little shops and a ton of food, in a studio apartment that overlooked the square where the music students played. I, on the other hand, lived next to an Indonesian corner store that had been robbed three times in my first month of tenancy, in a one-bedroom apartment that looked like a serial killer lived there. Hey, plenty of people didn't bother to decorate their apartments, especially when working on their doctoral thesis.

Regardless of my personal decorative failings, I sat in the many-times-patched red vinyl booth that every pizza parlor since time began has had.

Ben was late for our usual post-doctoral-meeting, I'm-never-graduating date, and it worried me. Of course it all came flooding back to me the moment it was dark out, and too late to contact David. I pulled my phone out of my black Hello Kitty purse and relaxed into the booth for a little Gmail. Maybe I couldn't call David at ten o'clock at night, but I sure as hell could harass him in other ways.

I sat with my thumbs poised over the screen. How could I even begin to explain what happened? How do you throw out "by the way, we had to shoot a slowly rampaging lion" into a conversation that ended three hours ago? Do you at least ask how the email recipient is before you traumatize them?

Dear David,

Backspace. Too personal.

Professor Barnes—

Too "I didn't do my homework" whiney.

David—

Like we're peers. Better.

We had an incident at the zoo this morning that I didn't get a chance to tell you about. One of the lions was behaving strangely—staggering, apparently having difficulty seeing, and an incredible resistance to pain.

David, I've never seen anything like this. She walked through an industrial strength metal fence until it almost killed her. We don't know what it is, but we had to shoot her when she shoved her face through the wire to get at her mate.

Dr. Warner, our veterinarian, thinks that it's a neurological disorder. The rest of us have no idea what's going on. Any ideas? Feline meningitis with a sprinkle of psychosis, maybe?

Any help appreciated,

Lens.

It was the best I could do under the circumstances. Hopefully, adding my lion dilemma to his to-do list wouldn't tip him over. If he drank one more cup of coffee, he might start to spontaneously levitate.

It took me a moment to recognize Ben. His black hair flew in every direction, with small tendrils sticking to the sweat on his forehead. He did not have the expression of a man that was looking forward to delicious pizza and great—okay, maybe just sarcastic—company.

"You look like glorified shit," I greeted him helpfully.

"I just spent three hours cleaning up blood and coaxing Luka into one of the concrete holding pens until we can figure out how to sedate him," he said, sitting down in the booth heavily.

"What happened?"

Ben shushed me quietly, much to my chagrin, as

the waitress approached and took our order. The moment her back turned, I pounced. "Ben, what *happened*?"

Ben closed his eyes and rested his head in the palms of his hands. "I wasn't at the staff meeting because Dr. Warner and I were trying to deal with Sahala. We finally loaded her—" His voice cracked and broke, and he swallowed hard. "Her body into his truck. Dr. Warner was helping me clean up the blood when Luka came over to the fence."

I frowned. "Came over like, to mourn his mate? To find out what was going on? Because blood is tasty to lions?"

"A combination of the last two, I think," he said. "He started trying to eat the wire. His eyes were cloudy like Sahala's were, and it was pretty obvious that he couldn't see. He tried to use his claws to cut through the fence, but he kept slapping at it, like he couldn't control his movements. So he kept growling—this weird, high-pitched growl—and biting it instead."

"What happened then?" I asked, leaning forward and spilling a jar of Parmesan with my cleavage. Classy.

"Then we had to use the catch poles and push brooms to herd him down the tunnel. We had to use the emergency siren to make sure no one came down. And Lens—

"This is the weird part. He was bleeding from his mouth from the wire, stumbling, and his knees kept locking up on him. He should have been terrified—he's only been in that tunnel unconscious for vet checks. But the only way we got him to move . . . Well, it was an accident."

"Would you just freaking TELL ME what happened?" Patience, party of one.

"I had been using the push broom to move the blood and water toward the grate, while Dr. Warner tried to sedate Luka and coax him toward the door of the tunnel. But he kept pacing, back and forth, in front of . . . where she did what she did. Finally he started to bite at the fence again, but at floor level."

"Near the broom," I said, finally catching on.

"Near the broom," he confirmed. "He followed the broom the whole way to the isolation rooms. The lights didn't bother him, the sirens—nothing. He was walking like he was on a tightrope—one foot lined up with the other—and he staggered the whole way down the hall, but he followed it."

"That's . . . gross and maybe romantic," I said finally.

Ben shook his head. "I feel like he would've followed even if the blood wasn't hers."

"So not romantic then. What else?"

"It gets weirder," he said heavily. "Once we got

him in the holding pen, it was like he turned off. He didn't pace, didn't attack the walls—he didn't even lay down or go toward the three pounds of chicken we put in there to coax him in. Nothing. He stood there and stared at the door. I checked on him after we finished cleaning and he was still there, just staring."

"What the fuck?" I said, leaning back against the booth. "Dr. Warner better put a rush on this necropsy. Maybe it isn't too late for Luka, but it sounds like it's getting close."

We smiled at the waitress and pretended that we weren't talking about dissecting animals, and I got my pineapple pizza and honey BBQ wings. The silence was punctuated by the sounds of contented eating until Ben cleared his throat.

"So how did your meeting go?"

"Weird also," I admitted. "For once I didn't get sidetracked, even by the thing I *wanted* to get sidetracked about, so we mostly stayed on topic. Except—did you hear that now they're saying everyone's susceptible to this flu thing, not just babies and the elderly?"

He frowned, which was quite a feat with half a slice of double mushroom pizza in his mouth. "No, I haven't checked my phone all day," he said. "So what does that mean?"

I shrugged. "I don't know, Germ-X your silverware at restaurants? Don't let people hack all over you? I assume it means normal flu things. David's worried, and he looks terrible, though, which makes me a little nervous," I admitted. "The CDC sent him samples of last year's flu and are sending him this one so he can compare and figure out what's different and how to create a vaccine. It seemed more important to talk about that than weird lion behavior at the time . . ." I felt badly, then, that after Ben had gotten so choked up and upset, I hadn't even thought to ask David about Sahala.

Ben nodded slowly. "I can understand that, I guess," he said. He paused, in that way that guys have that screams BIG TALK and that both of us should now become extremely uncomfortable. "I wanted to talk to you about something."

Nailed it. "That's never a phrase that's good to hear." I frowned as something caught my eye. As I looked over Ben's shoulder, I noticed it was a man at the front of the pizzeria, staring in my direction. I had never felt happier to see a drunk dude in my entire life. It gave me something to look at other than Ben's hopeful face.

"No, that one's 'we need to talk.' Hopefully, this one will go better than that." He paused again, meaningfully, and I wondered if I bumped the cheese with my boobs again that he'd leave our perfectly fine, undefined relationship alone.

"I think we should move in together," he said finally, fishing a key out of his pocket and sliding it across the table. It was zebra-patterned, of course, with one of those little plastic covers on it in the shape of a heart with a "L" in the middle. It was beautifully corny, I had to admit.

It took several seconds for my brain to catch up, and a few more for me to not answer with a bowl full of snark. "Like, together?"

"You're only at your apartment when you run out of clothes or my Xbox annoys you," he said, disturbingly reasonable. I knew what deer in headlights felt like. It wasn't terror—it was the absolute certainty that the absurdity of life had found me, and now that I was aware of it, Murphy's Law was going to bitch-slap me in the face. I just knew it.

"Fuck," I said simply.

He looked halfway between crestfallen and perplexed. "Me, you, or in general?"

"I feel like I've found the next level of adulting and I'm not sure what to do about it," I admitted. Living together meant something. It meant commitment. It meant that this was real. It meant that I could no longer get Cheerios naked at 3 in the morning without being chased by a penis.

"So . . . you don't want to?"

"I think I do? Maybe? But—Ben?"

He sounded frustrated. "Am I keeping the key, or—"

"Ben?" I said again, a bit more urgently. I couldn't help myself from glancing out the window to check on the progress of the drunk guy; usually they were college students and good for a laugh when they were out in public. Somehow, this was different. He hadn't moved.

He hadn't moved an inch. He was standing at the window with the glare of neon lights illuminating his face, his pale skin green and red under the bulbs. The man was staring straight at me, and though I couldn't see his eyes, it almost looked as if he wasn't really blinking, either. Something about him made the hairs on my spine tingle.

He noticed the change in tone. "Wait, what is it?"

"There's a guy staring at me through the window behind you. I thought he was drunk or something, but now . . . he's kind of giving me the creeps."

Ben turned slowly and looked at the man. He was wearing a green flannel shirt and jeans, regular build, brown hair—I felt like I should catalog him in case I needed to pick him out of a lineup later. As I shifted in the booth his eyes came into focus; they looked strange, as if he had cataracts or some other disorder. It tugged on the forefront of my memory; I'd seen eyes like those recently, but I felt like it was more important to stop Ben from going out there with a spatula than it was to remember why it seemed familiar.

"Ben, get a waiter or something," I hissed. "I'm pretty sure meth people bite, and we've got enough problems, tetanus won't help!" I'd upgraded him from drunk to meth-head. Something wasn't right, and I couldn't pinpoint it. I almost expected him to start pounding on the window, one heavy fist at a time, until the glass shattered and he could come after me. There was menace there, a malice that I hadn't noticed before—something about him made the caveman part of my brain begin to scream, and I knew I was in danger if we went outside. Hell, maybe even if we didn't go outside.

Ben opened his mouth as if he had a brilliant comeback, then snapped it shut. "Good point," he conceded, and got up. I didn't want to be One of Those People who can't help but check their phones every five minutes, but it was easier to check my damn phone to see if David had emailed me back than it was to watch Ben was have a stiff, whispered conversation with a waiter whose English was definitely his third or fourth language. As he came back and sat down, I sighed and shoved the phone back into Hello Kitty.

The waiter took a moment to steady himself, patted his apron flat, and threw his shoulders back. Evidently, dealing with potential meth heads was something one needed to prepare himself—gird one's loins, if you will—for. I watched him walk outside and approach the man who wouldn't look away from me. He seemed polite at first—then insistent as the flannel man continued to stare, motionless. He was motionless until he wasn't; he turned slowly, stiffly, until he faced the waiter. His movements were broken, as if he were the Tin man and needed a good oiling. He was rusty, and all I knew was that I didn't want him anywhere near me.

"Ben, I think I want to leave," I said quietly.

The waiter was exclaiming, throwing his hands in the air and speaking quickly, touching the man's shoulder and then pushing him, forcing him away from the window. I was suddenly worried that Ben and I were going to become witnesses for a pizza-room brawl. The man stared at the waiter for a long time, his hands grasping, open and closed, open and closed. I was certain that he was about to attack the waiter. I didn't want to go out there, and I prayed to Bob Ross that there was a back exit to the pizzeria somewhere.

The man finally broke eye contact with the waiter and blinked, shaking his head slowly. He began to walk away unsteadily, staggering and leaning against the walls of the shops that lined the street as he went. I watched until I couldn't see him anymore, and a tremor ran down my spine, finally.

"What . . . the hell," Ben said, turning back around to face me. I didn't have a good answer; I didn't know what the hell had happened, and I wasn't sure that I wanted to know. Was this some new kind of drug that I didn't know about? Was he just a weird perv looking for a giggle? Or was this something else, something that I should have recognized?

The waiter came back, looking unsettled. "Boxes?" he offered hopefully.

"Please," I said, and put my hands in my lap so that no one would see them shake.

#

We sat in my car with the doors locked and the windows up. Ben had walked to the pizzeria from his apartment, but we both seemed to feel a need to have some fiberglass and metal between us and the world. I touched the window lightly, feeling the cool night air against the glass, and closed my eyes.

We stayed in the parking lot well past when the

late night dinner rush was over. It was a 24-hour pizzeria; we weren't worried about being booted, but the nearly empty parking lot made my skin crawl. I watched the numbers on my dashboard clock climb and couldn't think of anything appropriate to say.

"So, not to be the asshole that puts off a somewhat traumatizing experience in favor of self-interest, but I'm pretty convinced that if this shit just happened on my street with the street lights blazing and college students drunkenly singing Adele songs in the middle of a pizzeria, you're not going home to the rat hole disguised as a ghetto that you call your neighborhood," he said finally, staring at the gray brick building in front of us.

I stared at him. "Really? We're finishing this now?"

"Just tell me that you're not ready, Lens. Tell me that you don't feel the same way I do. You should know by now that I l—"

He frowned as his work phone rang. At eleven thirty at night. On a Thursday. "It's Marley," he said, and picked up the phone.

Marley was a sometimes member of our little group; she was the herpetology specialist, and whenever the mouse or chicken or whatever she was currently feeding her snakes or lizards was too big for them, she liked to use a handmade trebuchet to launch it into the cat or fox enclosures to see what would happen. Regardless, that didn't mean she'd call us at eleven thirty at night to throw rodents at lions.

"Wait, I don't understand," he said slowly. "What happened?"

I sat on my hands impatiently, rocking back and forth. Clearly something had happened at the zoo, and it only took a moment of looking at Ben's face for me to put the car in drive and head toward the outskirts of town, toward the zoo. Relationship talk be damned (yay!). As I listened to half a conversation about Luka (didn't seem good) and Bacon (only Marley would name an African Rock Python "Bacon"), I put my foot on the gas. Something didn't seem right—not that anything seemed right at the zoo lately. David and meth man forgotten, we sped on into the night, and I prayed to Bob Ross that when we got there, we wouldn't need the shotgun.

Day Three

Indecently Early

I probably should have invested in a small arsenal, in retrospect.

It was after midnight by the time we got to the zoo, and the maze design of the habitats had never frustrated me quite as much as it did then. Sometimes we just wanted to get where we're going without visiting every exhibit—and when you're in a hurry, the amount of locks and keypads to make it through the "short" way made it feel like the zoo gods were against you.

We skidded to a stop at the offices and knocked on the back door to the snake house where Marley's prized incubators were kept. She wasn't a fan of letting other employees into the herpetology habitats—who knew that snakes were so fragile?—but calling us in the middle of the night, when darkness touched twilight, probably gave us permission to bust the door down.

Marley was much like her snakes. She wasn't one to panic, or even to show outward emotion—but damn, she moved when she had to. She was nowhere to be found when Ben and I hit the door, and in my face in the next moment. Her bright gold and red hair was thrown back in a messy bun held in place by the tongs used to feed snakes frozen treats, and her green "I work at the zoo, ask me anything!" jumpsuit was splattered with . . . I didn't want to speculate on what she had on her, actually.

Ben stopped short and bounced on the balls of his feet nervously. "You don't usually keep yourself in the know about the cats," he said abruptly. "What's going on? All you said was that Dr. Warner hadn't gotten back to us on the necropsy, that there's something wrong with Luka, and that Bacon's acting funny now."

Marley said nothing, but simply led us over to the back end of Bacon's habitat. We didn't have a LOT of snakes and lizards, but the ones we did have required enough care that Marley was a busy woman. She was also in charge of snake and lizard breeding for other zoos across the country. Marley was good at her job—so good that it took me several moments to find Bacon, because his habitat matched him perfectly.

Bacon was an African Rock Python, one of the largest snake species in the world—and from my beloved continent. Thankfully, he wasn't venomous, but at a humongous fourteen feet long, the zoo had its work cut out for it trying to feed him. It always felt wrong that I couldn't immediately spot a fourteen foot long snake that almost weighed as much as I did. Snakes like that should be obvious, Hank-colored and terrible at hiding, just to give people a fighting chance of not getting a leg constricted.

Bacon was perfectly obvious once I found him—it was the finding in the first place that was the hard part—as he lay coiled in his swamp beneath a broken log. His next-door neighbor, a fat monitor lizard named Lincoln, was nowhere to be found, which was normal. What wasn't normal was that Bacon was striking at the wall—the reinforced thick wall that kept the snake from eating its natural prey—over and over again.

I watched as his scales shivered, rustling together restlessly. His musculature bunched and contracted beneath them as he prepared himself to strike—and when he did, my heart sank. African Rock Pythons were fast—maybe not the fastest snake out there, but fast enough to catch an antelope—but Bacon was striking with the speed of our Morning Risers 60+ speed walkers club. The little old ladies “power walked” at the grand speed of one mile an hour around the zoo for exercise, and made massive donations to the zoo for the privilege. Either way, the strike was slow enough that he faltered, his head dipping and hitting the log as he worked to mash his head against the gray wall next to him.

Bacon was hunting—poorly—at something that he had never known was there before today. He was suddenly aware of Lincoln’s presence, through the wall, in a way that he never had before. Marley let us into the holding habitat so we could get a closer look. One of Bacon’s impressively long fangs had splintered and broken and he was bleeding from the mouth; his scales were bent and ragged near his fangs.

The worst was his eyes.

His eyes had the same strange cloudy miasma that Sahala’s had, that Luka was beginning to have. I’d never spent a lot of time staring into a snake’s eyes and wasn’t entirely certain what color they were supposed to be, but I was fairly sure that wasn’t it.

“He’s been doing that for two hours,” Marley said quietly. “I can’t get him to stop and I don’t have anything with soft walls to keep him in. I fed him a chicken laced with sedatives and it didn't touch him. I heard the gunshot earlier and figured something was wrong—is this what happened to Sahala?"

Ben closed his eyes and leaned back against the thick Plexiglas. "That's almost exactly what happened to Sahala," he said. "She started going after Luka the exact same way—sluggish, uncoordinated, and seemingly unable to feel what she was doing to herself. Her eyes looked the same way, too."

"It can cross species," I whispered.

"What?" Ben turned to look at me.

"Whatever this is, it isn't isolated to one species. *Everything* is at risk for this now. Sahala's habitat is nowhere near Bacon's, and somehow he's acting the same way. We need to act like everything between the lions and the snakes are possibly contaminated, and we need to figure out how this transmits, soon." While the Quagga was extinct from poaching, not from disease, I'd at least hung around with David enough to know about viral vectors and the likelihood of certain viruses to cross species. This was rare—and in this case, rare was bad.

"Crap," Marley said simply.

"Crap," Ben echoed, rubbing the bridge of his nose with his middle finger. I was almost positive it was coincidental, and not a statement at the universe. "What did you say about Luka, and why are you the one who knows about it? No offense, but you usually stay in your snake box."

"Dr. Warner called and left a message at the research center while I was over there visiting Hank and stretching my legs," Marley said, leading us back toward the incubator room and locking up Bacon. The sound of his snout hitting the habitat would haunt me for a while yet. "He said the necropsy is taking a lot longer than he thought it would, that he's having to cross-section her brain. He wasn't clear on why, but he asked for Ben to keep an eye on Luka, because he'd never seen anything contagious that acted this way. So I went to see Luka." She busied herself with heating up pieces of chicken and dead mice and rats for her snakes, dunking them in hot water and waiting for them to thaw.

"And?" I asked.

"And he's still in the isolation room staring at the door," she reported with a sigh. "At least, I assume that's what he was doing when you left him there. It didn't look like he'd moved much. The only time I saw him move was when I opened the hatch to see if he was making noises or anything."

Ben frowned. "You aren't supposed to open the hatch," he said slowly. "In case of accidental contagion or injury."

"Now I know why," Marley said dryly, putting the

meat in various cups and bowls to be stuffed with vitamins and other nutrients that kept our snakes healthy. "Something about this has to do with smell. It's the only thing I can think of. There's no way that Bacon can see Lincoln—but he's acting like he can *smell* him through the wall. Did you see how he stopped and scented every couple of seconds? His tongue's damaged, but he's still tasting the air. And when I opened the hatch to check on Luka, the second my face got close to the door, he rammed it with his head."

"He rammed the door?"

Marley nodded. "Like his life depended on it. He lunged into it over and over again, just like Bacon's doing. He was walking funny, so it was almost like he was falling face-first into the door, but I'm pretty sure that's what he was doing."

"Crap," Ben said again.

"I think we've all decided we're fucked, Ben," I said, sitting down on one of Marley's stools. I closed my eyes, trying to think. This was so out of my depth that it wasn't even funny. The whole world was going insane, and I didn't know what I could possibly do about it. Somehow the responsibility of the zoo had fallen on the shoulders of the cat guy, the intern, and the snake chick. People in charge didn't usually stay at the zoo after midnight. We were on our own.

"We're going to check all of the animals, separate anyone who's trying to eat their friends, put contagion signs on the habitat doors, and try to convince the boss to close the zoo tomorrow," I said finally. "I can't think of any other way to contain this. We have to use the emergency holding cells. It's not like we have padded rooms for lions or something."

Ben eyed me warily. It never boded well for him when I was in decision-making mode. "This is gonna be a long night, isn't it."

"On the bright side, it's technically already morning."

Marley smiled brightly with a large dead rat in her hand, stuffing it with fluorescent green vitamins. "On the brighter side, it isn't my job," she said cheerfully.

"Crap," we said. At least we were in it together.

#

No matter how many times I did it, it was always spooky going through the zoo in the dark. Many of our most dangerous animals were nocturnal, and hearing the hunting and other noises they made at night was mildly terrifying. A zoo emptied during the day was a quiet park full of sleepy animals; a zoo at night was alive, with gorillas grunting and nearly talking to each other, wolves howling to each other through the darkness, and the alligators hissing into the night. It was a cacophony of nightmares, and my caveman brain tingled unpleasantly as we walked.

Ben and I began at the start of the zoo, with the koalas. I'd brought a notebook to track who was trying to eat who; there had to be a pattern to this somehow, and it was up to us to find it. The koalas were peacefully in their trees, staring at us as if accusing us of having the audacity to intrude upon them during nap time.

The foxes were in their dens, but I didn't see any dirt flying or fur being pulled out. More importantly, there was no blood anywhere that my flashlight could shine. The red pandas were just as offended by our presence as the koalas had been. Then came the tigers and the wolves, and every hair on my body stood up at attention.

I wasn't as familiar with tigers as I was with lions—Ben had his favorites, as we all tend to do, but I'd heard enough to feel sort of responsible for them as well. Ben came up behind me as I watched the tiger habitat and laid a hand on my shoulder.

"I wish I'd gone into virology," I said quietly. "Nothing's going to change in the world if I improve or stop the Quagga project, but a possibly new disease that can cross species? I feel like I can't do anything to stop it."

"It's not like you could have predicted this when you picked your major and fell in love with Africa," Ben reminded me. He fumbled with his Official Zoo Flashlight designed to help keep us from blinding helpless zoo animals. We peered at the habitat, and I marveled again at just how well wild animals could blend in. A 450-pound orange striped cat didn't seem like it could disappear into the greenery, but there we were.

There was an electrified fence between us and the habitat. Back in the day, the zoo had a concrete gulf in front of the habitat—but when Benji, the male tiger, jumped the shit out of it to get at the peacocks that roamed the zoo freely, the zoo realized the error of their ways . . . and to never underestimate an animal's desire to pluck pretty tail feathers. The animals with the electric fences all knew that they were there without testing the limits, as if they could hear or sense the electricity; we'd never had an accidental injury.

We might have an accidental injury tonight. I straddled the wooden barrier that kept patrons away from the fence and hung there awkwardly. "Um, a little help?"

Ben was staring at me like I'd just shaved my head. "What the hell are you doing?"

"Trying to find a giant fucking tiger in the pitch black, and I can't see from back there," I said.

It turned out that I didn't have to climb the barrier.

As the little fence was trying to relieve me of the ability to bear children, and I struggled to complete my "hop" over, I stopped. Visions of Jurassic Park and the water glass in the truck flooded my mind. Leaves crackled, one step at a time, in the darkness of the tigers' "forest."

The back of my brain screamed for me to run. I could hear strong, predator jaws snapping at the air. It suddenly seemed like a good idea not to move.

Benji stalked forward through the bush. I sat quietly, my pants straining to rip on the barrier, and didn't move my little pocket flashlight. As he came into the halo of the dim, discount battery light, I could see that he was limping.

I watched in horror as Benji dragged his back right foot behind him. It was mangled, the bone turning his foot out away from his body, blood staining his large orange paw. A glint of white flickered in the flashlight beam. He began to growl, so low that I couldn't hear it—but I could feel it.

His eyes were cloudy. Whatever this was, it had found the tigers.

Benji continued his slow march forward, the bone

in his foot tip-tapping against every rock he passed. He wavered as he walked, swaying like a drunk, and reared back on his one good leg.

He launched himself at the electric fence.

"Oh my God," I said, and fell off the barrier. I scrambled backwards flat on my ass, ducking under the wooden fence and running into Ben's foot. I smelled what happened before I saw it; sparks flew and there was the scent of burned fur as Benji fell back to the ground, his paws smoking. He roared, a hoarse, throaty sound, and reared back once more. As he hit the fence again and shrieked, I shoved Ben backward as far as I could, crawling to follow.

Benji had electrocuted himself. No, correction; Benji was *continuing* to electrocute himself, trying to get to me, as I scrambled under the fence. I heard the crackling and the thick thud of his bulk against the metal as I stifled a scream, finally managing to get myself out from under the barrier I'd fallen off of.

That was how I discovered the insanity had a radius of about six feet. Once we were far enough away from the habitat, Benji stood still on raw and smoking paws, staring at nothing, unmoving and barely breathing. He stared at me with his dead, dull eyes, with nothing of himself left in them, and I couldn't bring myself to break away from the sadness of his gaze.

My hands shook as I pulled out my notebook to make note of Benji's behavior. I dropped the pen once, twice; Ben helped me up from the ground and pulled me tightly against his chest. I could hear his heart pounding, and wondered if mine was thundering to match.

"What the hell is happening?" I whispered, and felt wetness on my face. I was convinced it was beginning to rain until Ben tenderly wiped the tears off of my cheeks.

"I don't know," he said simply. "But this has to stop. Let's get the list done as quickly as we can, stay away from the habitats, and then we can divide and conquer."

"Divide and conquer?" I rubbed at my eyes, embarrassed at the display of emotion.

Ben nodded, staring at Benji over my shoulder. "I'm getting in touch with the boss and waking his sorry ass up whether he likes it or not. We're closing the zoo tomorrow. I'm going to have Marley call all the other keepers in that work day shift to come help us on nights to catalog this shit and find a pattern."

"What about me?"

Ben grasped my hand and led me toward the wolves. His hand was slick with nervous perspiration, and I'd never felt so happy that someone else was as scared as I was. "You're going to go to Dr.

Warner's house, and email David until his phone wakes him up."

"I've never wanted a man's phone number quite as badly as I do right now," I said.

Ben offered a strained smile. "Me neither."

#

It hadn't been since my undergrad days that I'd pulled up in a strange man's driveway at three in the morning. At least this time I knew I'd come out of it sober, as much as I might regret that decision. I had the creeping sensation that we were missing something, and that a slumbering Dr. Warner and likely still-studying David were the key.

I took a breath and walked up the inexpertly landscaped pathway. Peonies and small rose bushes haphazardly decorated the cobblestones, with glow-in-the-dark pebbles sprinkled throughout to light the path up to the cabin that had a ceramic dog, holding a bone that said "welcome." The only other decoration was the modest veterinary symbol on an old-fashioned shingle over the carved wooden door.

I took a breath and hoped he wasn't a heavy sleeper. I jingled the Pandora bracelet on my left wrist that Ben had given me for Christmas (bet no one could guess that it had a zebra print bead prominently displayed); my only real, adult jewelry—and sighed. The sound of the jingling only soothed my frayed nerves so much.

I began to swear quietly, pacing back and forth on the small wooden porch. The guilt I felt at needing to wake up Dr. Warner warred with the concern of what might happen if I didn't. I threw myself down on his porch in the darkness and rested my head back against the rough logs. Maybe Ben, Marley and I were overreacting. Maybe this wasn't as bad as we thought. Maybe—

Dr. Warner wore pancake boxers. I knew this because he stumbled out of his front door carrying a cheese stick and looking somewhat disheveled. "Lens, why are you sitting on my porch?" He paused. "More importantly, how do you know where I live?"

"I know where Jeff keeps his Rolodex at the zoo," I said quietly. "We're fans of Rolodex . . . es."

He walked down the porch barefoot and sat next to me, staring out into the night. "I'm going to assume that something bad happened."

I closed my eyes, playing with the two beads on my bracelet. I longed for when my life was simple: Quagga, Ben, and visiting my herds of zoo animals. How did I wind up in the middle of a veterinary disaster? "You could say that. How did the necropsy go?"

He hesitated and offered me a cheese stick. I knew a distraction when I saw one and stayed silent, watching him. "It definitely had something to do with neurology."

"Well, that was informative."

Dr. Warner grimaced. I realized that I'd never learned his first name. "I was up in my lab slicing her brain into histological microtomes for analysis when my front door camera came on and I saw you cursing Hell's nipples on my porch." He glanced at me. "No smile? I'm not smiling either." He paused, staring at a rustle of softly waving grass. I sat next to him, my brain struggling to keep up.

It was peaceful here; I could imagine deer chewing softly on the grass each morning as the sun rose. It was somehow comforting to think that life went on even in the midst of such chaos and tragedy.

"Her brain . . . had changed consistency in key locations for motor skills and higher cognitive function," he said carefully.

I stared at him for a long moment. "What the hell is a microtome, and . . . changed consistency? Can we perhaps be a bit more specific, and dumb it down?" I'd never met someone more capable of reducing me to a gibbering pile of imbecile than Dr. Warner.

"Microtomes are those paper-thin anatomical

slices that you see in museums. And her brain was rotting while she was still alive. It was as if moths had eaten holes through it. I have no explanation, nothing at all. I'm sending samples off to a colleague that specializes in infectious diseases for exotics. He'll get it by morning." He rubbed his eyes. "Later in the morning, anyway."

I watched what I hoped was a rabbit slink through the grass and dandelions. I felt unmoored here; disconnected from the panic, my thesis, Ben and the Quagga and my real life. If the word "idyllic" could describe a real place, this would be it. Dragonflies flitted from plant to plant and suddenly the beauty of it all had me in tears. It was all too much; everything was too much.

"What's wrong, Lens? Besides the obvious." He rested a warm, slightly cheese-stained palm on my shoulder, looking more than a little concerned.

I resisted the impulse to throw my hands in the air in frustration. I closed my eyes, refusing to acknowledge the wetness gathered beneath my eyelids. "Whatever it is, I think Lenny and Carl have it, and Bacon, too. It's crossing species, Dr. Warner, and I don't know what to do. I'm just a geneticist in training." My voice cracked, and I winced.

He sat back against the cabin, staring out into a night rapidly fading into morning. "I'll check on them when I get there," he said finally. "But I want you guys to start gloving up and wearing masks when you deal with your animals."

I blinked slowly. "Why?"

"Because if this thing is jumping species, it might not be long before one of us gets it," he said grimly.

I could have really used a drink.

Day Three

Still Early, but Manageable

I drove aimlessly around town after leaving Dr. Warner's house until I found an all-night Denny's. French toast and grilled cheese would cure at least a few ills, and I hadn't eaten as much of my pizza as I'd have liked. As I sat back in the scuffed green booth, I pulled out my phone and stared at the thin, hairline crack in my Fancy Tempered Glass Protector. I really needed to replace it; wasn't that the whole point of the protectors, to crack for your screen? I started to navigate to Amazon and flicked through a few different types of screen protectors. It wasn't until I somehow found myself on the Essential Oils page that I realized I was stalling.

I glanced at the clock on my phone. Four a.m. Dr. Warner would be getting ready to go to the zoo, and

I had a feeling I would want to be there, if I could. I hesitated with my thumb over the Gmail icon and switched over to CNN.

□□ Headline News □ Flu Strain Called "Potential Epidemic" by German Scientists; America Declares Flu Strain "Beatable" □ Citizens are Cautioned to Wear Masks in Public □ Vaccine in Progress □□

Well, shit.

The fact that America was calling it "beatable" meant nothing to me. We had a history of saying that nothing was wrong when the world was blowing up around us. It was the "potential epidemic" that gave me shivers. I looked around Denny's carefully, examining each patron to see if any of them looked feverish, and then gave up, realizing I wasn't even close to being a medical doctor. I had a hospital mask from when my mother thought we were all going to die of H1N1 and mailed me a few from Wal-Mart; that would have to suffice.

I sighed and opened Gmail to David. *Get on Facebook messenger. Or text me. It's not like you don't have my phone number somewhere. You've got to be awake by now, right? —Lens*

As my French toast slid onto the table and I smiled at the waitress, who undoubtedly thought

I was insane for eating both French toast and grilled cheese at the same time, I opened the "compose" screen again. *This is an emergency, David. Something's seriously wrong at the zoo.* I paused. *And what the hell is going on with this flu strain, anyway? They're saying it's serious. What, are people throwing up until they die or something?*

I switched over to messenger and began to text Ben. *What's going on at the zoo?*

Managed to convince the boss that electrocuted tigers weren't good for business. Zoo closed for the day due to "revamping habitats." May have threatened him a little. Not sure if I still have a job, but am at the zoo anyway.

Ben was one of the most prolific texters I'd ever met. He always seemed to feel as if it were necessary to text his entire life story. His auto-correct must be insane. I vowed to look at his phone the next time we weren't in the middle of a crisis.

Dr. Warner is coming at five. Trying to wake David now.

It occurred to me that there were still such things as phone books—and more importantly, whitepages.com. I knew David's first and last name; I knew roughly where he lived; and I had an hour to figure out which David was him.

Thankfully, there weren't as many David Barnes

listed as I thought there would be. I prepared myself for getting screamed at at least a few times and began to dial numbers.

One nervous (presumed) mistress whispering at the phone while a wife screamed in the background, one old man that was remarkably cheerful and told me all about the eggs and sausage he ate every morning, and one sleepy, confused man later, I found an equally sleepy and confused Professor. I could tell that he'd been up late after I'd seen him; he sounded exhausted, and I almost felt bad for waking him.

"I really, really need you to get to the zoo. Like, by five."

"Lens? What the hell? How did you get this number?"

I paused. Were we really so tech-savvy that we forgot numbers get listed? "Um, I looked it up. It wasn't that hard. Though I do think I interrupted a weird domestic squabble trying to find you. If you don't want students calling you at"—I checked the time on my phone – "four thirty in the morning, you should work on getting unlisted. Look, the point is, we had a tiger try to electrocute himself, two jaguars trying to eat each other and NOT in the good way, and a snake trying to burrow a hole through a wall to eat his neighbor. I don't know what the hell is going on, but you might, so go get your pants on and meet us and Dr. Warner at the zoo by five." I paused again. "And please don't let this affect my thesis."

I hung up rather quickly after that.

#

As it turned out, a morning person David was not. We met Ben, Dr. Warner, Marley, the rest of the animal techs and keepers, and Jeff in the aquarium office at five that morning. Most of us were used to waking up that early, but the nighttime keepers looked a little rough around the edges; they usually left around four. Ben had done some serious convincing to get this many of us together at one time.

Dr. Warner looked significantly better in jeans and a blue button-up shirt, rather than pancake boxers and a white tee. He also looked like he hadn't slept since this whole thing had started. He cleared his throat and helped up his hands, calloused by years of working with heavy-duty veterinary tools, and lifting stretchers full of 500+ pound animals. "Quiet, please." He gestured to Ben.

Ben sat down on my rickety desk. "So it's fairly obvious at this point that you've been lied to, right? Enough people heard the gunshot, the lock down sirens, or the gossip by now to know that something freaky's going on?"

Marley interrupted. "Not to mention that some of us never come out of our proverbial boxes, so the fact that we're all here and not with our animals means that we're royally fucked."

Ben sighed. "Mildly fucked. Yesterday, I had to . . . shoot Sahala after she . . ." Ben paused, looking a little green.

Dr. Warner picked it up from there. "She had a neurological event that caused psychosis, an almost complete resistance to pain, and the desire to attack her mate," he reported quietly. "Those of you that knew her know that that's not like her, at all. I performed a necropsy last night and spent most of the late night and early morning examining her brain."

He took a deep breath and looked at David for a long moment. I frowned. My stomach clenched uncomfortably as two of my professional circles collided in ways that I didn't know how to deal with; I didn't know Dr. Warner and David knew each other.

"I believe that this is a virus, and I'm not sure how it's transmitted. Three more species have begun to have symptoms since yesterday. We know it's not blood-borne or transmitted through bodily fluids, as one of the animals is housed behind two inches of security glass," he nodded at Marley. "I just don't know what to tell you. I sent off a sample to a friend and I'm waiting for a response."

"There seems to be a lot of that going around," David muttered, "except I'm the friend." I nudged him hard to get him to shut up.

Dr. Warner looked at a loss; defeated, almost. He was the one we all ran to for answers; he knew everything in the zoo world, or so we thought. There wasn't anyone else to go to, except his mysterious friend. "All I can do is wait with you. I'll try to keep the animals showing symptoms comfortable, and Ben and Lens are going to help everyone quarantine every animal we can. If we keep everyone separate, maybe we can stop this thing." He went quiet for a long moment, staring at the fish tank.

It was still peaceful; no symptoms there, no bloody fish or sharks trying to break the glass. Wasn't *that* a terrifying thought. It made me curious, though, to know what was so different about the fish tank that hundreds of different types of fish and other animals could live together and not one would have begun to show symptoms.

Something was different about the fish tank, I had a feeling. Something that we were overlooking. I watched one of the sharks glide by, blissfully ignoring the presence of the humans that he could easily take legs off of, and wondered what the hell I was missing.

#

Ben and I began—well, at the beginning: the koalas were by the front gate, and we started there. We had enough concrete kennels—or habitats, or quarantine cells—for pretty much every animal in the zoo, behind their real habitats. The keepers and trainers worked on the animals touching big orange targets on poles with their noses; at least, the dangerous animals were trained to do so, and we could use that to get them to follow us through the facility. Thankfully no one has ever been eaten by a koala, so we went into the habitat and lured them into the kennels with leaves.

The foxes were another story. We gloved up and wiggled raw chicken strips in front of their dens, hoping that at least one of them would come out, but no dice. We set the chicken by the exit to the back habitats and hoped that eventually hunger would lead them to where we needed them.

The red pandas followed, and then there were the tigers.

Lilah was dead.

Lilah was very dead, and my worst nightmares were coming to life. Benji had stopped smoking from the electrocution, but the fact that he was relatively in one piece didn't help the fact that Lilah wasn't. Benji was standing next to her, unmoving, staring off into the distance.

Her belly had been torn open, and there was nothing left inside.

I had never been so thankful for the buckets that were ever-present for every task under the sun in a zoo. They made a rather tidy space for me to throw up my French toast in. Ben was swearing creatively at the entrance to the outdoor habitat, watching Benji stare, watching the inside of Lilah's body steam with released heat. He was stuttering as he cursed.

"I can't believe he ate her," I said finally, after the grilled cheese had followed the French toast.

"I can't believe we didn't see it coming," he said numbly, closing his eyes. "I have never been so relieved to have the zoo closed. No one should see this. No one should ever have to see this." He choked and followed my path to the buckets.

I wasn't sure what he meant, that we didn't see it coming. Did he know something I didn't? Was there an illness that suddenly clicked for him that I was unaware of? I sighed, running my fingers through my hair, and tried to stick the touch pole between the bars in the door.

Benji would normally come bounding in, booping the touch target with his nose as hard as he could for his treats. It was his favorite trick—it scared the hell out of new keepers and overjoyed onlookers. Benji had always loved attention.

Benji didn't love anything anymore.

Benji wasn't home. I couldn't see anything in his beautiful, wild eyes. I couldn't see a spark of intellect, personality, whatever made him, him. He simply stood there next to the body of his mate, blood dripping off of his jowls, as if nothing had happened.

"What in the hell are we dealing with, Ben?" I whispered, wiping my mouth with the back of my hand. I stared at Benji, wondering what it would take to make something so devoted to his mate do something like this. I didn't know about the mating habits of tigers, but I knew that Benji and Lilah had something special. This was not the kind of special I thought they'd had.

"When we're done quarantining the animals, you're going with David and Jeff," he said roughly. "David said that his friend would get the samples later this morning, and Jeff might be able to help him figure this out. This has to stop. What is this, the zoo-pocalypse? This can't be happening," he muttered, closing his eyes.

The wolves were next.

Day Three

Respectable Hours

It had taken until almost noon to quarantine all of the animals. Every keeper and tech helped, taking care of their section of animals, until we finally felt confident that we'd contained this thing. The final tally was that the birds, the chimps, the zebras and other herd animals, as well as the giraffes, were not showing any symptoms. The coyotes, gorillas, and brown bears were starting to look a little squirrely around the eyes. The other keepers were working hard to quarantine "their" animals when I left.

Jeff, my zoo supervisor, had decided to pull out his Big Science Degrees hat and work alongside David to examine the brain tissue that Dr. Warner had lent us. I wasn't sure what the two of them could accomplish together, but it had to be better than Ben, myself, and the rest of the zoo techs, half of which decidedly did not have degrees in this type of thing.

As I followed Jeff and David back to the college and pulled through the vine-covered archway, I realized that my tunnel vision wouldn't serve me very well. Clearly my thesis was on hold for the duration; that wasn't a problem, but I had to stop viewing things as "helping thesis" and "not helping thesis." The thesis had been such a large part of my life for so long that it was hard to let go of, even temporarily. Moving in with Ben? That was a discussion I could put on hold, too; it disturbed me to realize that I genuinely was on the fence about moving in with him. Moving in meant Commitment in a Big Way, and I wasn't sure we were ready for that kind of thing.

Even though we practically lived together anyway. It was the principle of the matter.

When I looked up across the parking lot and saw one of the football players staring at me, though, I began to feel uncomfortable, and realized that a zoo crisis was not license to stop paying attention to what was around me, or to ignore things that felt "wrong" to my caveman brain.

"Take a picture, it'll last longer," I shouted. I felt like I was back in middle school, but it was the best comeback I had, under the circumstances. His lip was twisted in a strange smile, and his dark eyes followed the length of my body up and down as I walked across the parking lot toward the building. Something about him made me walk faster, and I realized I'd left my pepper spray in the car. A chill ran down my spine, and I remembered the man outside the pizzeria.

A zoo-pocalypse in the making and I had to worry about football player rapists. Great.

The halls were oddly silent, and the students and faculty I did see were hurrying past each other, looking fearful. I frowned. The news had said that Europe had been hit pretty badly by this flu thing, but we were just meant to be prepared—it hadn't actually gotten to us yet, I'd thought. So why was everyone so worried?

When I got there, David was behind his microscope again, and Jeff was buried behind a pile of books. Research was His Thing; it was his passion, and he mostly researched zoological information—especially regarding the health and wellbeing of exotics. It was part of why he was the coordinator for my program; he knew a little bit about everything, and if you were interested in animals or animal genetics, he was the man to go to.

"So why am I here again?"

David pushed a microscope in my direction

without looking up. "You took Biology 101, didn't you? Look for what doesn't seem right."

I frowned again. Obviously I'd taken an obsessive number of biology courses, but that didn't mean I was suddenly an expert on squishy brain matter of animals. I sighed and sat down, looking over at Jeff. "What are you looking at?"

He didn't look up, either. I felt completely and totally important and needed at that moment. "Historical diseases in exotics, zoos and circuses, to see if this has happened before."

That made sense. I took off my glasses and looked through the microscope at a tiny slice of Sahala's brain. I stared at it for a long moment, trying to conjure up what brain matter was supposed to look like—it was like a tiny dimply minefield, if memory dredged up the correct pictures.

Or I Googled it under the desk while Jeff and David weren't looking, either one.

This brain tissue . . . was not that.

It looked like melting glass. The little dots on healthy tissue were smeared together and ran down the slide, turning black as it went. It looked like her brain had dissolved.

"Tell me spontaneous cranial combustion isn't a thing," I called out cautiously. "Because this kind of looks like a bomb went off?"

David snorted. "I'm waiting for Dr. Warner's specialist to answer that one."

"If we're waiting on a specialist, why are we doing this?"

David sighed. "Half because Jeff's better at academic research than I am and I felt a need to try and help, half because I don't want to think about the samples the CDC gave me, and a sprinkle of 'let the doctoral student learn something' in there for good measure."

I turned to look at him. "You're sitting on the CDC samples and aren't sharing?"

"Yeah, David, why aren't you sharing?" Jeff taunted from behind a zoological journal from 1936.

He hesitated, drumming his fingers against the tabletop. "Because they don't exactly take 'classified' lightly."

The hairs on the back of my neck stood up. "David, you *have* to tell us."

"The flu virus reached the U.S. two days ago and shut down a small airport in New Jersey. That's all I know. I can't even get a list of symptoms. Nobody is talking about this thing." He looked away, his eyes sliding across the black table as he stared blankly into space.

"Which means it could be serious," I muttered.

There was no way he'd have *that* look on his face if it wasn't serious.

"Which means it's probably serious," he echoed. "I'm guessing it's upper respiratory like the rest of them, contagious as hell, and everyone at the airport panicked when they started coughing on each other and hacking up mucus on the tarmac. I'm hoping it's the hysteria that's bad, not the disease."

His eyes strayed briefly toward a stack of slides and paperwork and I frowned. I wasn't an expert in espionage and spying, but I knew damn well when someone was lying to me. He was clearly covering something up, and knew more than he said he did. The question was, what?

When it rains, it pours, I thought. I had to trust that David knew what he was talking about, even if it seemed sketchy now. I sighed and turned away from the microscope. "Look, this clearly isn't my forte. It's fun and all, but I'm already in over my head just doing damage control at the zoo with Ben. If you find a genetic component for susceptibility or something, then I can be useful, but for now, I think I should go be a nuisance at the zoo or try to help Dr. Warner."

David eyed the CDC sample again for a split second and cleared his throat. "That sounds like a plan," he said vaguely, and went back to his microscope, without looking up. Jeff didn't so much as grunt. It was nice to have taken a random drive all the way to the college just to be told I wasn't needed.

I walked quickly to my car, but I didn't see the creepy football player. I debated stopping for tacos on the way to the zoo, but I realized I probably couldn't eat as many as I wanted before I got there, and I sure as hell didn't have the bank to buy enough for the whole class. I sighed and turned the radio on with the satisfying 'click' that newer cars just didn't have, settling in for the longish drive.

" . . . and it looks like the long-awaited flu has finally hit America, folks. I'm getting reports of it all down the Jersey shore—but who needs the Jersey shore, anyway?" I grimaced as the DJ laughed. He wouldn't think it was so funny if he was bending over the toilet coughing his guts out, half-dead with pneumonia. "Look for your friendly neighborhood flu symptoms—fever, chills, coughing, the works—and proceed to your doctor or nearest hospital. And as always, indulge the germaphobe in you with Purex hand sanitizer, brought to you by . . ."

I closed my eyes, then realized I was driving. It *sounded* like a normal flu—but then, why was the CDC so concerned? And if they were concerned, why weren't they telling everyone what to do?

That nagging feeling in the back of my brain brought me back to thoughts of the aquarium. After

I parked behind the offices, I rushed to my desk in hopes of inspiration hitting me in the face. Or sharks. Sharks hitting me in the face sounded better than thinking about all of this.

That was when Marley came in to tell me that Bacon had escaped the Dead Box.

Day Three

I Should Be Eating Lunch Right Now

The Dead Box was located behind Marley's snake enclosures and workroom. She normally stored mice, rats and various pieces of chicken in it to feed her snakes; occasionally, a large black box sat in half of the huge freezer and held a somewhat smaller deceased animal waiting for Dr. Warner to perform a necropsy, usually reptiles, small mammals or birds.

It had a lock on it only because the state mandated that it should; truth be told, Marley never bothered. It was one more step in an already complicated day, and really, what was going to escape a deep freeze when they're already dead?

The answer, evidently, was an African Rock Python named Bacon.

Ben and Marley stood staring at the freezer while I more reasonably spent my time staring at corners, waiting for Bacon to pop out and try to kill me. "So we don't know where he is?"

"Nope."

"A giant snake? A giant snake that killed himself trying to eat a monitor lizard through a wall that had a steel plate in it, was beginning his journey to deep freeze his little ass off, and somehow managed to not only wake up, but open a sealed, if not locked, freezer with his broken skull and slither his not-so-little way out and into the room, and we're just standing here?"

Marley didn't look up from her contemplations of the freezer. "Yup. That about sums it up, actually."

"Crap," I said. It was beginning to become my word.

Ben shifted his feet and crossed his arms, staring at the open freezer. The big black box that was super-refrigerated or magnetically sealed or powered by X-Men that Marley kept deceased animals in was also open, and it had a dent in it. Ben swallowed hard. "We're sure he's not still in here?"

Marley turned slowly, leveling her gaze upon him. She stared at him for one lingering, uncomfortable moment.

"Right. The next stupid questions are, are you sure

he was actually dead? And who the hell do we call about this?"

We didn't exactly have a head zookeeper. Two of the department heads were currently together in a stare-down with a freezer, and it had already taken Ben threatening him for the owner to close the zoo for a day. I couldn't make myself believe that he'd have any answers here.

As Ben and Marley argued, I sank into a corner. I wanted my dad in the worst way. He would have known what to do. He'd been an exotic vet for over 30 years when he'd died. He was one of the original reasons I went into zoological genetics in the first place. If anybody would have been able to tell me what to do, it would have been him.

I fell further into feeling sorry for myself and rested my forehead on the palms of my hands. There was something going on here that was so much beyond me and my paltry experience; something that I didn't even begin to know how to deal with. I could feel tears welling in my eyes as I thought about Sahala, and Lilah, and Bacon. Evidently, that was a cue—it was then, as I sat prone and not paying attention, that he found his moment to strike.

Bacon was definitely back.

I felt it before I saw it; his mangled jaw was thankfully too broken and twisted for him to clamp down on my arm. It took me several moments to catch up with the fact that the pain radiating from my elbow wasn't from a bite.

It was from bone.

"I found him!" I shrieked, and twisted my arm to look. Pieces of skull dug into my flesh, blood spreading around the fragments like a kaleidoscope. In slow motion, I saw him rear back for another strike.

My heart sank as I slid across the wall to try and get away. His eyes were clouded, his movements jerky and uncontrolled. He had a dent the size of my fist in his face, and I could see a large, stained fang dangling loosely from his jaw.

"Where?" Ben and Marley said together.

I kicked a trash can between me and the giant snake. "How about you both get off your asses *and come and find out*?"

It wasn't that I was afraid of snakes—far from it. I'd helped Marley plan countless presentations, watched baby snakes hatch with pure joy, and I'd even handled Bacon once or twice; he was Marley's favorite, and everyone met him eventually. The problem was that I had a healthy respect of what snakes could do—and one who had evidently pulled an Easter Sunday on us was something far out of the scope of my experience.

It would have been funny if it wasn't so sad; I

could almost see myself scrambling in the corner with—oh, man.

That's when it hit me. "They're fucking *zombies*," I said with awe.

"They're not zombies," Marley said, as she dove across the room and grabbed Bacon at the base of what was left of his skull. "There's no such thing as zombies." It wasn't a conversation I ever expected to have with someone that had tears rolling down their cheeks and a giant snake in their hands.

"But there is something really wrong with him," she grunted softly as she wrestled with him. "We need Dr. Warner. Now."

I dusted myself off and grabbed the large metal carrier that Marley transported venomous snakes in when she did presentations. If that didn't hold him—two layers of thick, reinforced steel with steel bars between them for good measure—nothing would, and we'd be screwed anyway. Marley lovingly coiled the still-attacking Bacon as best as she could with Ben's help; I felt like I'd do more harm than good trying to shove a not-a-zombie snake in a box.

Marley collapsed on the floor, staring at the ceiling for a long moment. I simply sat next to her, touching the back of her hand. It was like losing a pet, except they were still alive-ish, and obviously not well. There was a cancer in Bacon that was consuming him—maybe not literally, but there was no denying that something was driving this terrible behavior, and we were going to run out of time eventually. We had to figure this out before we were keepers of nothing but air.

#

Dr. Warner was evidently a busy man. He had already separated the jaguars, and they stood calmly, staring at nothing, in their individual pens. I was currently laying on my back on an office chair, spinning around upside-down, staring at the aquarium in front of me. Ben had gone to tend to his other cats; the tigers still weren't looking that great. Hank chose that moment to saunter by, and I frowned. Hank was also a cat. Granted, they were entirely different kinds of cats, but he was still a cat, and it seemed like the cats were getting nailed pretty hard by this sickness. But Hank was fine.

What was different about Hank? My brain buzzed with the need to find meaning in the difference. Something was afoot here, and I didn't know what—but Hank, the aquarium, and the weird split between affected animals and not affected animals meant something, something important.

I checked my email while I lay prone in the chair. Of course, there was no news from David yet, but Jeff had sent a quick message saying he was coming back to the zoo. I couldn't help but think we were forgetting something—something important. I sighed. The twin worries of Hank and the mysterious "forgetting something" were plaguing my brain. It was right out of reach and I knew it.

I just hoped I would really "know it" before it was too late.

I got up and wandered back to Marley's cave to check on the situation with Bacon. Actually, I was more checking on the situation with Marley; she hadn't said anything when we'd left, and I knew that Bacon was hitting her hard.

"How's it going?" I found her rearranging the bedding around some about-to-be-hatched snake eggs, meticulously placing moss and leaves around them.

Marley remained quiet for a long moment before she reached over and turned the music down. I didn't know what she was doing until I heard it.

Thump. Thump. Thump.

Bacon's carrier was on the floor near Marley's station. Every few moments, I saw the box jump and heard the thud of Bacon trying to escape. I frowned. "Mind if I try something?"

"Anything," she sighed.

"Come help me." Together, we heaved the steel carrier over to the corner, between the dead box and Marley's desk. Bacon whipped himself into a frenzy as we moved, and I winced as I heard bone fracturing. After we adjusted the carrier, I dragged Marley about two yards away.

The thumping stopped.

Marley turned to me with wide eyes. "What the hell?"

"Benji tried to electrocute himself to get to me. I think that whatever's making them attack has about a six-foot radius. As long as nothing—presumably nothing matching their prey profile, since Benji wasn't trying to mutilate frogs or anything—was in that range, it's like they turn off or something. They just stop moving, like they're trying to load Windows 95 or something."

Marley frowned. "Maybe it's heat, or pulse. Or scent," she mused, drumming her fingers against a frozen rat. She stared at the Bacon box, contemplating where the hell we could put a fourteen foot snake that he wouldn't be surrounded by living things—it being a zoo and all.

That was when we heard the shot.

Marley and I stopped to look at each other for one brief moment before bolting in the direction of the sound. As we ran past the giraffes, coyotes and wolves, the lack of songs and calls chilled me. How many animals would we lose?

I skidded to a stop in front of the foxes, shoving open the viewing window. I heard screaming and cursing and my heart sank. What if Ben—

"Whoever that is, get the hell in here!"

I sagged in relief before letting Marley unlock the indoor habitat area with her set of keys. We opened the door cautiously to see a scene from a weird Japanese horror film.

Ben shot the rifle into the sky—I hoped against hope that was what we'd heard before—and Jeff was being eaten by a fox.

I wasn't one for gore. A detached part of me that wasn't screaming inside marveled at what subcutaneous and fatty tissue looked like in humans. The rest of me wanted to throw up, but I hadn't gotten the tacos TO throw up. The thought at least distracted me for the half a second I had to grab a catch pole before Marley opened the gate.

Marvel and DC were our mating pair; we were waiting on news that she was pregnant. It looked like DC wasn't going to be getting anyone pregnant any time soon. He wasn't growling or shaking his head to "kill" his prey—he was trying to eat Jeff.

Jeff's face was a pale white tinged with blue and

he was breathing rapidly, panting "fuck" over and over again as DC dangled from his forearm. Marvel was hissing and pacing on the other side of their den, as if she knew that she wanted to have nothing to do with his shit.

Blood was rushing down Jeff's arm, pooling in his clenched fist. I held the catch pole and charged, swinging wildly at DC. I wanted to try and knock him off if I could; something, anything to stop the grating sound of teeth against bone.

"You're making it worse!" Jeff howled as DC's mouth worked continuously against his flesh.

Ben yanked the pole out of my hands and braced his legs. He waited a moment even as Jeff fell to his knees, screaming. The timing was perfect—as DC swung forward, clamped onto Jeff's arm, Ben hit a home run—knocking DC unconscious.

As DC fell to the ground, a thick chunk of Jeff's flesh, the circumference of a baseball, went with him.

That was when Jeff finally lost consciousness and fell onto the leaves, blood rushing out of his body with every beat of his heart.

"Shit!" Ben whipped his belt off in a move Indiana Jones would envy and used it as a tourniquet. I thought that there was almost no way a doctor could fix such a gaping hole; it was entirely possible that

Jeff could lose his arm, especially if we left the tourniquet on for long.

"Should I be doing something to secure the possibly rabid fox?" I asked.

Marley shoved me out of the way and grabbed the catch pole, securing DC away from Ben. "Go get Dr. Warner," she said through clenched teeth. "And call an ambulance or something!"

I ran, fumbling with my phone to call Dr. Warner. I barely let him answer the phone before I shouted "Where are you?"

"Examining the alligators for signs of disease, since we couldn't get them out of the pond to quarantine. Why, what's wrong?"

"Jeff got bit and it's bad. We need an ambulance."

"Why the hell did you call me first?"

"I don't know! You're a vet, I figured you could keep him alive until the ambulance got here!"

I heard the sound of his feet hitting the pavement and stopped, waiting for him to come into view. After a few terrifyingly long moments, I saw him.

"Thank God!" I said.

He frowned as we jogged back toward the foxes. Before we hit the entrance, he stopped me. "I'm beginning to wonder if we shouldn't call an ambulance," he said tentatively. "At least, not yet."

"Why the hell not? A tourniquet is not a solution!"

He grabbed my hand as I reached for the door. "This might be the best chance we have of finding out if this thing is zoonotic," he said apologetically.

"What do you mean?"

"I mean that if he consents, I can probably patch him up for long enough that he could become one of the most important case studies in zoological history."

"You deliberately want to keep him here to see if he gets infected?" I'd never understood the phrase 'my jaw dropped' until I felt it happen.

"If he doesn't, keeping him in a tourniquet means that his arm might be toast anyway, so as long as we pump him full of antibiotics and I see if it's an injury we can keep a lid on for a while, he might be fine for the night. If he does get infected, I'd rather it be here where we can put him in a quarantine room so he doesn't hurt anyone else the way the animals are."

I felt sick. The scientist in me wanted nothing more than to see this through and figure this out. The rest of me was screaming in terror.

"Let's ask him," I said finally. If it were me, I would want to wait and see. If we were on the verge of the biggest discovery in zoonotic history, there was no way I would err on the side of caution.

I only hoped we were wrong and would need to

come up with an excuse for why we let a vet doctor him up and why we didn't call an ambulance immediately. Otherwise, this was about to get ugly, and fast.

#

We moved Marvel into her own habitat, and DC went into one of Marley's snake boxes. Jeff was the only one rooting to be an experiment, though that may have been blood loss and brief unconsciousness. Marley and Ben, however, put a simultaneous foot down.

After two hours of arguing and a very long response time from the ambulance, we watched from the back gate as one of our own was carried off, fate unknown.

"He's probably going to lose the use of that arm, if not the whole damn thing itself," Dr. Warner said, as the ambulance drove off into the stereotypical sunset. "DC got a good chunk of muscle mass. That doesn't exactly grow back."

"Shouldn't we warn them?" I said. "That he might . . ." I couldn't finish my sentence. Couldn't even finish my thought. There was no way that I could imagine Jeff attacking the paramedics.

"No," Marley replied, clenching her fists. "This is a zoo problem. There's no way it's going to pass to him, it's bizarre enough that it's crossing animal species. Besides, he's got enough problems; they might not be able to fix the hole. God knows what they'd do to him if they thought he had some weird disease."

It was then, with the early autumn sun setting and the rest of the day keepers getting ready to leave, that we heard it.

The owner had called the ticket booth manager, Mary, and Mary had called the staff to let them know the zoo was closed. Ben and Marley were going to take care of notifying the night staff. What we didn't remember, what had been plaguing my memory all day, was that it was the first Friday of the month.

The day that the volunteer crew took over the ticket booths and stands, and the Junior Explorers took over the zoo.

The sound of excited children rose throughout the zoo as we stood staring at each other. It was Marley who managed to call out, "The blood in the habitat!" as she raced off toward the foxes.

The foxes, who were one habitat to the left of the front door of the zoo.

Ben and I took off running.

Day Three

Dinnertime Went So Wrong

Ben and I didn't have gate keys to the zoo—or, rather, gate codes. Only four people had the codes: Mary from the front office and the owner for the daytime shift, and Jeff and the volunteer coordinator for night. There was no way to stop the kids from coming in—they were already there. We couldn't exactly kick them out without causing a panic. And the volunteer coordinator always locked the gates to make sure that children didn't wander out into the countryside.

We ripped through the zoo and grabbed the covers we used when habitats were down, working together to put the tarp that stated "Our animals must be hibernating! Come back soon!" in bright letters onto the hooks above the glass. As the children's instructional seminar ended and the "adventure" began, we heard them begin to troop through the zoo, running wildly in every direction.

Panting and leaning back against the tarp-covered glass, Ben looked over at me. "How long before they realize that all the animals aren't just 'hiding,' they're gone?"

"Shit." I rubbed my eyes. "We have to fix this. How did none of us remember this was happening?"

He glanced at me sidelong as we began to jog back toward the aquarium and offices. "We've had a little bit on our minds the last few days."

As we reached the offices, I could hear the outside lights click on. Darkness fell on the zoo. Children were laughing and chasing each other, and I could hear the volunteer moms (and dads!) murmuring to each other as we passed through the aquarium. Apparently, at least a few people had noticed . . . well, the lack of a *zoo*.

The volunteer coordinator had apparently figured it out, because she clapped her hands for attention. "Explorer troops, fan out across the zoo and find your remaining troopers! We will reconvene at the food court in ten minutes!"

"They really take this seriously," I remarked to Ben. I unlocked the door so we could hide behind the aquarium. Ben flipped through the Rolodex to call Mary, and Dr. Warner took that moment to walk through the door. The poor man looked exhausted.

"No luck?"

He slumped down in a chair and closed his eyes. Hank immediately climbed onto his lap. Traitor.

"The only things I can think of are mosquitoes. I can't imagine what else the animals that have this have in common." He frowned at Hank. "Does he ever go outside? Could he have been exposed?"

"He's a glorified house cat. We can't trust him to roam the zoo alone. This one time—"

Both my phone and Dr. Warner's went off at the same time. Mine was an email from Jeff:

I think it's zoonotic, Lens. It's hard to remember stupid things like my email password right now. My limbs feel really heavy and I don't really think I need the morphine they're giving me. Something's happening. This hospital is full of flu patients—I have a feeling I'm going to get something, one way or the other. Report back. Keep me sane.

I looked up as Dr. Warner's eyes met mine. "That was my exotic vet friend," he said slowly. "He works at a zoo in California. He said that they were beginning to find the same problems . . ." He paused. "Did you happen to change meat distributors recently?"

I frowned. "Nice segue. We switched to Pierson for the animals and I'm pretty sure we switched suppliers for the food court, too. Why?"

"Are you aware Pierson owns the largest national meat distributor plant in the continental US?" he persisted.

"What are you getting at, Doc?" I asked.

Marley came out of the woodwork, looking from Hank, to the sharks, and back to Hank. She stood quietly for a long moment, staring into the dark abyss of water, watching the shark I'd taunted only a few short days ago swim lazily past sea turtles and fish. It was so peaceful; so unlike the rest of the zoo.

"Hank eats cat food," she said slowly.

"Yes, Marley. Very good. Hank eats cat food," I replied, rolling my eyes. "What the hell does all of this have to do—"

"No—Lens, Hank eats CAT FOOD. I feed my snakes mice, rats, and chicken—Bacon was the last one to eat, and he got a huge chunk of the new batch of chicken from Pierson. What do the sharks eat? What did Sahala eat?" She began to pace, rubbing her temples with her fingertips.

Dr. Warner smiled sickly and closed his eyes, saying nothing. I frowned, staring into the tank, and Ben dropped the Rolodex. "Oh my God," he whispered. "You're right. Sahala preferred chicken over beef. Benji, too. Are you saying—"

"Every animal that I've seen today that exhibited symptoms was a carnivore," Dr. Warner said quietly. "Every one. And I'm willing to bet that every single one of them gets chicken in their meals. It's in the chicken. It has to be."

Ben turned away from the aquarium slowly. "What did you mean when you were talking about Pierson being the largest distributor? There can't be enough zoos that that's all they do."

"Pierson is just a brand name for the animal meat they package. The whole company is known as Levonn. They have several plants—two for pre-packaged large and exotic animal meat, and several for human-grade and quality meat products. It's the same chicken," he added. "They just treat it different ways. Separate facilities, same chickens."

Ben sat up straight. "We use the same company for guest meals, too?"

"You and a whole lot of other companies. It's—"

"Marley, call the front desk, see if Mary's still there. Tell her to make an announcement to close the food court and then call the kitchens. Have them shut everything down. Hurry!" Ben grabbed me by the hand and started to run to the door.

Marley frowned, picking up the phone. "I know this is bad, but what—"

"There's kids in the zoo and they're at the food court!" he shouted. "Come on!"

Dr. Warner and I tore after him. I had a sneaking suspicion that this was not going to end in our favor.

#

We stopped running when we hit the gift shop that sat on top of the food court stalls. Children in mini zoo keeper outfits milled around, throwing food and laughing. My stomach sank as I saw amongst the hot dogs and hamburgers another quintessential childhood food—chicken fingers.

"You don't really think—" I began tentatively.

Ben gently took my shoulders and turned me to face the flamingos that peacefully hung out in their pond next to the food court. Dr. Warner stood at the window, staring down at the children. Two little boys and a little girl stood painfully still, watching the flamingos. One reached plaintively toward the birds, rocking his body against the chains that separated flamingos from humans. The stillness of the others reminded me of the football player when I'd gone to the college.

I looked up at Ben. "It's not the flu?"

“It’s not the flu,” he echoed.

“Are we really saying contaminated chicken is causing the zombie apocalypse, and we’re in the middle of—” I paused, counting. “Over a dozen types of very large, carnivorous animals?”

Ben bit his lip and sighed. “There’s more.”

“What more could there possibly be?”

He gestured at the volunteer coordinator. She—and two more little explorers—were slowly stumbling toward the koalas. “We sent home, hospitalized, and now zombified everyone with the key code to the gates.”

“Wait, what?”

“Jeff, Mary, the owner, and the event coordinator. Jeff’s at the hospital and the owner’s at home. The event coordinator is about to eat a koala . . . and I hadn’t looked at my watch lately. It’s after 5. I doubt Mary’s still here.”

“Are you sure?”

“I’m not positive, no. It’s *just* after five. It’s worth a shot.”

Dr. Warner stayed quietly in the corner of the gift shop, watching the children. Empty plates and containers littered the food court; everyone had already eaten in the amount of time it had taken us to figure this out. We were too late, if this was really happening.

"Coming, doc?"

"Not yet," he replied quietly.

Ben and I left him in the gift shop and made for the front office. I frowned. Something wasn't right. The way Sahala and Benji reacted with their infection was different from how the football player and the guy outside the pizzeria had acted. Maybe Jeff would be okay after all. Maybe we were wrong, and it was just a particularly virulent strain of salmonella.

I felt somewhat hopeful as Ben knocked on the ticket booth/office door. Surely Mary would know how to get the healthy kids out, how to call their parents; things far adult-ier than my limited life experience had allowed me to figure out. Mary was a no-nonsense grandma that adopted all of us zoo denizens as her own. She would know what to do.

I knocked Ben aside with my hip and opened the door. "Mary, please be here. We're in deep shit—"

Hands closed around my throat, fingernails digging in and burying themselves in my skin. My chest immediately felt like it was going to explode; I grabbed the wrists of the person holding me and tried to scream for Ben. My vision faded slightly as the hands squeezed. Ben was so beautiful in this blurry world; he moved so slowly.

The floaty feeling collapsed in on me as I saw Mary's dentures coming fast for the side of my face. I shrieked as Ben wrapped his arms around her waist and pulled hard.

Saliva dripped onto my cheek, warm and wet. It was thick and viscous, the texture of maple syrup. I gasped as her hands tore away from my neck; I could feel her fingernails sliding from my skin.

Ben fell backwards with Mary in his arms. They flailed together, Mary's dentures snapping wildly, her arms still reaching out for me. Ben wrestled determinedly, and I scrambled for the maintenance closet behind Mary's desk.

My eyes found the extinguisher and the fire axe near the maintenance door. Every fiber of my being screamed "zombie apocalypse!" and wanted to grab the axe—but this was Mary, the woman who baked custom-flavored brownies for each of our birthdays. I reached for the gray roll of duct tape on the closet shelf and hurried back to Ben.

Mary's teeth were thankfully on the ground next to Ben, who sat on her lower back, holding her wrists down. "You read my mind," he said grimly. "Hold her while I tape her up."

I took the moment to grab a handful of tissues and wiped the cooling globule of spit from my cheek before it dripped into the wounds on my neck. I thanked God and Bob Ross and anyone else out there that I was enough of a biologist to not have a major panic attack that I could magically acquire . . . whatever type of disease this was through intact skin.

I straddled Mary and held her arms—probably a bit harder than necessary. She did, after all, try to eat me. Ben wrapped about half a roll of tape around her wrists and tied her shoelaces together for good measure. He noticed me staring and gave me a small smile.

"I heard a joke once about a funeral home that tied their clients' shoes together, just in case," he explained, sitting back against the wall. He closed his eyes and sighed. "Okay. So it's not like we're stuck here permanently—it would be a fire hazard. There has to be a physical key on the property."

"Probably in John's office," I replied. "But I think our bigger problem is the fact that we have about forty kids and parents loose in a zoo with no animals and diseased chicken."

Ben carefully placed Mary in her office chair, leaving her dentures on the floor. It was probably better that she didn't have them, really. I felt like I was handling the situation quite well until Ben came over and gently touched my throat. "You're lucky you don't need stitches." He paused. "On second thought, you could probably use some. We should go find Dr. Warner."

"What the hell," I managed, and laid my head

against his shoulder. A tear streamed slowly down my cheek and hit the wounds on my neck. I winced and pulled away. "This sucks. This really fucking sucks."

"That's one way to put it," Ben murmured over the sound of Mary's gums snapping and the low, moaning growls escaping her throat. "But you're right. We have to do something about the kids."

I closed my eyes, thinking about my Quagga. Maybe one day I could resurrect a dead species. One day I could move to Africa and watch the herds run through the brush. One day I would know exactly what to say to Ben to let him know how I felt, and we'd live happily ever after in the savanna, watching lions eat my zebras the way nature meant for them to.

This was not that day. Today was the day that lions tried to eat each other and worse; today was the day that children grasped grubby hands at flamingos with longing looks. Today we had a mission. But first . . .

"I really think I need stitches," I winced, and sighed.

Day Three

Twilight Time

We made our way back to Dr. Warner, who had remained behind to watch the children and their parents. He looked at me for a long moment. "Does the gift shop keep a first aid kit in here?"

Ben made his way behind the counter toward the storage room as I sat down in front of the large viewing windows. "Did anything happen while we were gone?" I asked.

He shook his head, accepting the kit from Ben and rummaging through until he found some Betadine. "We've got to round them up. It's a closed circuit; if we locked the doors to the aquarium we could keep the infected children and adults in the outer ring and put the others in the aquarium with us. I'm sure there's a parent list in the volunteer coordinator's bag."

I paused, taking a deep breath as the iodine hit my skin. “So what you’re telling me is that after Mary tried to eat me, you want us to go find the volunteer coordinator, who looks an awful lot like she’s infected, and pry her purse from her greedy little hands without getting attacked again?”

Dr. Warner closed his eyes with a sigh, grabbing the small suture kit that was in every zoo first-aid kit. You never knew when a rogue goose would try to eat a staff member. “I was going to ask Mary out on a date,” he said mournfully.

“That’s . . . really not an appropriate topic of conversation when you’re 30 years apart and she tried to attack me,” I said. I jumped as Dr. Warner touched the needle against my skin; once, twice.

Dr. Warner poked me again and I nearly fell off the table I was sitting on. He gave a Manly Communicating Look at Ben, who went back to the store room and returned with more duct tape. “Now we know that Lens is a wuss,” Ben added cheerfully. He offered the duct tape to Dr. Warner, who began to use it like butterfly stitches. It would probably stay a hell of a lot better than they would, anyway.

“A tiger tried to eat me through an electric fence and our office manager just tore my skin off with her fingernails. Can I be entitled to one modicum of freakout please?” I refused to obey the urge to smack Dr. Warner's hands away, but it was a close call.

Ben sighed, scrubbing his eyelids with his fingertips. "Okay—the game plan is to quarantine the ones that are acting weird in the outer section, away from the aquarium and away from the quarantine tunnels for the animals. Dr. Warner and I will take care of that part. Can you and Marley handle bringing the other kids to safety?"

"I feel like you're treating me like a fragile little flower," I muttered. "I can handle this. I can handle more than this. I've got this!"

Okay, the adrenaline of the attack might have been making me a little woozy.

Dr. Warner eyed Ben as he started to pack up the first aid kit. "*I* feel like you're volunteering me for things that I don't want any part of," he replied. "Not that I think I get veto power in this situation. I just wanted to register a complaint."

"Complaint duly noted," I said dryly, slowly standing up and waiting for the dizziness to subside. I thought I was handling this situation fairly well, all things considered. My own personal panic attack was blossoming internally quite nicely, and I was able to keep a lid on it as we walked down the stairs toward the seating area. Handling little kids was definitely not my forte—there was a reason I wanted to move to Africa. Well, many reasons, but one of them being that I wanted absolutely nothing to do with children. How hard could it be, though, really?

As I opened the door, I heard a raspy growl. Small, grubby hands opened and closed as they reached for me, clumsily clamping around my wrist before tugging hard.

I fell back like a shot and ran butt-first into Dr. Warner as I slammed the door. "The little explorers are cannibals!"

Ben stared out the window as three more children stumbled toward the door. "This is ridiculous," he whispered incredulously. "This is seriously the zombie apocalypse. In a zoo. With miniature zombies. What the hell are you supposed to do with miniature zombies?"

"I fucking TOLD YOU SO," I snarled, ripping the door open to the kitchen. I rummaged through drawers and cabinets until I found what I was looking for, and presented oven mitts and cookie sheets to the men.

"What the hell are these for?" Ben asked.

"Gloves and shields, duh," I replied, mittening myself up. "I'm not paranoid enough to think that the virus is living in their fingernails, but I don't want to take any chances on getting their saliva into fresh wounds. We don't know what the hell this thing is."

"She's right," Dr. Warner vindicated me. "It's entirely possible that it can be transmitted through saliva. I cannot believe we started the zombie apocalypse with fried chicken."

"I want to know what the hell the government was experimenting with," Ben said. "Antibiotics and GMOs didn't do this." He paused, frowning. "Did GMOs do this?"

I stood there with my cookie sheets, listening to them debate, and smacked Ben in the chest with a piece of metal. "I'm betting David can answer that better than we can." I raised my voice over the banging of small fists against the door. "Why don't we ask him AFTER this becomes more of a philosophical exercise and less like the local Scout troop wants to attack us through a door!"

Ben brandished the cookie sheet I'd shoved at him like a shield and opened the door. A volunteer rushed up to take the children, looking more than slightly concerned. "I'm so sorry, I don't know what's come over them!"

Ben touched her arm gently, pulling her away from the door—and the children. "We need your help. Round up all of the kids that are okay, and bring them to the aquarium. This is Eleanor; she's going to come with you and lock up the aquarium to make sure all of the kids and volunteers stay safe. Dr.

Warner and I are going to call the parents of the . . ." He hesitated, glancing at us sidelong. "The sick kids."

"Some of the adults are acting strangely, too," she said nervously. Her hands absently plucked off a child's grasping fists from her sweater. "They're just not responding to anything I do. Mrs. LeDoux is just standing there, staring at the koalas! I don't know what to do, she's supposed to be in charge!"

"I'm sure it's just the flu," I said in an attempt to be soothing. "I heard it hits you just like that." I snapped my fingers loudly to demonstrate.

Twelve heads shot up and children, three parent volunteers, and Mrs. LeDoux began to walk toward us at the sound, step by slow step. The child pestering the girl talking to us seemed to . . . *scent* the air, somehow.

I grabbed the girl by the arm—I think her name was Kelsey, or maybe Katie—and hauled her forward, beginning to babble in an effort to distract her, and everyone else, from what was going on around us. "Explorers' club, right? All right, Explorers! My name is Eleanor, and my job is to take care of all of the herd animals at the zoo! Why don't you all follow me to the aquarium, but first, who can tell me what a herd animal is?"

About fifteen hands shot up, and an additional six kids began to follow. Three or four parents looked grateful as they gently began to shoo their children in the direction of the aquarium. Four or five more were urgently talking to children that were staring off into the distance, their fists grasping and opening reflexively, over and over again.

I looked back at Ben helplessly. This was going to be a disaster, and soon. He simply nodded, and I realized that I had to trust that he'd handle it somehow. I had my job, and he and Dr. Warner had theirs. Nothing was going to get done if I spent all of my time worrying.

Not that that would stop me.

I led the train of children with an unending stream of chatter, quickly walking past the empty exhibits. I could hear roaring, chittering, and banging behind the scenes; I walked a little faster past the carnivore exhibits, talking loudly about the differences between a prey animal and a predator.

I almost tripped over my own shoes as I realized that that distinction might change in this very zoo incredibly quickly for these children.

I held the doors as the children poured into the aquarium, quietly locking them as everyone filed in. I kept up the chatter as I crossed the aquarium to the other sets of doors, locking those, too. If Ben and Dr. Warner found stragglers, I was sure between the two of them they could figure out how to unlock a door and shove them in.

"And if you'll give me just a moment, I'm going to go confer with an associate of mine to make sure what our super-fun plan is going to be!" I hollered over the voices of the children. The aquarium had a tendency to calm people down; the parents looked less panicked, the children more excited. They almost looked like they could forget that their monthly trip to the zoo was turning into a weird disaster right behind their backs.

I hustled to the back offices. Of course the door to the stairway that led to John's office was locked—and his office itself was probably locked, too. For someone who never came to the zoo he owned, John was more than a little paranoid about the 'treasures' in his office from his various trips around the world. Swearing, I made my way to the herpetology center, praying that Marley was still there.

She was sitting approximately eight feet away from Bacon's box, angrily pressing a tissue into her nose and cursing at her tears. "I don't know what to do," she said, as she saw me come in. "All the big snakes are trying to eat their way through the walls. The big lizards—everyone who ate the chicken. All of my work . . ."

I sighed, rubbing my forehead. "If it makes you feel any better, I think everyone's work is going down the drain," I replied. "If the flu thing is the same as the chicken thing, we're sunk, Marley. This is huge. And we've got 30-some-odd kids in the aquarium and I have no fucking clue what to do with them."

She dried her eyes carefully, somehow managing not to dislodge her thick black mascara. "I've got some baby corn snakes that we can show them," she said slowly. "I was breeding for a specific morph, and—"

"Marley, I love you, but I don't think the kids are going to care about snake patterns." I paused, looking at Bacon's box. It was mostly quiet; every so often, I heard a disturbing "click." I frowned.

"Exposed bone," she said softly. "He's hitting his forehead against the metal wall of the carrier. But he's slowing down. Not hitting as hard." A small, twisted smile plastered itself on her lips. "I'm hoping that he'll stop for good soon."

"Ben and Dr. Warner are trying to round up the kids that want to eat each other," I offered. "And the parents that won't leave them. I'm not sure which group of us has the worst situation to deal with."

She stood slowly, pressing her hands on her lower back. "What are we going to do about the animals in quarantine? What if it doesn't hold?"

"Quarantine will hold," I said grimly as we began to walk into the nursery to gather up some baby snakes. "We don't have much of a choice otherwise."

#

As Marley settled in to play with baby snakes, excited children, and politely terrified parents, I grabbed my phone and checked my email. Jeff *and* David. This wasn't good.

It took me several moments for my biology and genetics degrees to kick in so that I could discern what the hell he was talking about:

Lens—

I always knew GMOs were an awesome idea, but I never thought we'd mess them up in such a spectacular fashion.

Basic Biology 401 – Levonn has been naughty. The CDC tested a lentivirus on their chickens in hopes of reducing the antibacterial resistance that they're passing along to humans. Lentivirus are always missing pieces to prevent activation—and our brilliant government agencies didn't realize that their current genetic modification programs included a helper virus with those missing proteins . . .

The new flu strain is *the flu—and it causes an immune response that helps activate the virus.*

Our saving grace is that you have to be exposed to the chicken AND the flu to activate it. It is the chicken, right? Dr. Warner CC'd me on his emails to his vet friend.

Lentiviral replication = mindless animals who want to infect everything they can find.

We created our own apocalypse, and I don't know if it's too late to stop it.

—David

Fuck.

Lens—

You haven't updated me. There's something wrong. The hospital is so quiet. My hands keep twitching and I can't stop it. What's going on? Where am I? Why am I here I don't

Double fuck. I scrolled through Jeff's contact information and dialed. The phone rang long enough that I worried that he wouldn't pick up. My worries were justified—he didn't. A nurse did—or someone who was acting like one.

"Can I talk to Jeff, please?"

"I'm afraid he can't come to the phone right now," she said politely.

"Why not?"

"Because Mr. Lorrey lost consciousness almost an hour ago and was transferred to the ICU. He appears to have limited brain function and is drifting in and out of consciousness. I'm so sorry, honey." Likely realizing how many HIPAA laws she'd just broken, the nurse abruptly hung up on me.

I frowned. Should she have even answered his phone? Some shady shit was going down at the hospital, and it made me nervous. I dialed again.

"Jeff?" I frowned. Who the hell had been in his room, then?

"Who is this?" Jeff's voice was gravelly, as if he hadn't spoken in years. He sounded suspicious, almost as if he didn't trust me—or the phone—who knew?

"Jeff, it's Lens. Eleanor, from the zoo?"

"What do you want? What the fuck do you want? Oh, God, Lens, I'm sorry. It's so hard to think right now. I'm so dizzy."

"What's going on?" I sat down outside the aquarium door in the office and rested my forehead on my knees.

"I don't know. Half the hospital staff is sick, a lot aren't even coming to work is what the guy who changes my IV said. There's candy stripers running around trying to act like nurses. Everyone has masks on and I haven't seen a doctor in hours, not since they tried to stitch up my arm." He moaned softly, and I could hear him shifting and turning on the bed. "I feel like the anesthesia's still got a hold of me."

I had a sinking feeling that the virus was transmitted through saliva after all. "Just hold on, Jeff. We're all trying to figure this out." An idea struck me. "What's the key code for the zoo? The volunteer coordinator locked the gates to keep the kids safely inside and we don't have the code."

He was silent for a long moment. "I . . . I don't know. I don't know, Lens! What's wrong with me? It's . . . it's 913 . . . 913 . . ."

That left four numbers, too many to guess. "Come on, Jeff. You can do it."

He snarled, and I heard the plastic frame of his phone groaning under the pressure of his hand. "I don't know! I don't know! I don't—"

"Mr. Lorrey, let's check your vitals," I heard over the line. Jeff shrieked "I don't know!" one last time, and I heard his phone clatter to the floor. Then I heard the screaming begin.

The virus had found Jeff.

#

In the meantime, the drama had begun to mount up. Ben had texted me; he'd tried to call the owner, to be told that only idiots would go out and expose themselves to the flu. He hung up on Ben before he could even ask for the key code.

Want to take kids + parents to infirmary, he texted. The problem was that the infirmary was near the exit—and you had to go through the aquarium to get there. *Download Zello, it's a walkie-talkie. Easier than calling or texting.*

Setting it to download, I sighed and pulled Marley aside. "Ben and Dr. Warner want to take the sick kids and parents to the infirmary," I murmured.

She pulled a baby snake out of her hair and handed it to one of the little girls. "So we need to move everyone?"

"Sounds like it," I said.

"We can put them in the nursery," she offered.

"Sounds like a plan. Ben's calling the parents with Dr. Warner. I think we need to call the police," I admitted. This is way outside my comfort zone.

Marley snorted. "Lot of good they've ever done me," she said, and clapped her hands. "Who wants to see more baby snakes and lizards?" she hollered, leading the kids toward the nursery.

I walked into the animal tunnels, which strangely had better reception than the aquarium, and hit the "emergency dial" button on my phone. It felt a little like I was doing something wrong; nobody had died or anything, but if you couldn't call the police for attempted cannibalism . . .

"911, what is your location and the nature of your emergency?"

"Cornerhouse Memorial Zoo, and I'd like to report—" What the hell did I want to report?—"an attack and several little kids with symptoms of that weird new flu." It was *technically* accurate.

The 911 responder sounded both sympathetic and frustrated. "You and the whole city," he said. "Please tell me this is the 'there's someone staring at me menacingly' type and not the 'my mom tried to attack my dad' type."

I swallowed hard. "A little of both," I hedged. "But we've got a lot of little kids here that don't have it, and the volunteer coordinator is probably going to start eating people."

"I'll put you on the list for a quick response, but it's going to be awhile," he warned. "We don't know what's going on, but it's happening across the whole county, and the ambulance crews haven't had a moment to rest. Good luck." And he hung up.

It had spread that far in the few hours it took David and Dr. Warner's specialist to figure out that it was the chicken. We were too late to stop it—but maybe not too late to warn others, I thought.

My resolve to salvage the situation rallied and I stuck my head in to call to Marley. "I'm going to break down John's door and look for the zoo keys. Can you handle the kids?"

"Sure," she called back.

I finally found a use for my fire axe—this one outside the door to the staircase that led to John's office. As I hefted the axe and contemplated minimal possible damage versus maximum my-boss-is-a-jackass satisfaction, I heard it.

My head snapped up as the growl rolled off of his tongue. Every hair on my body stood at attention. I knew that growl very, very well.

Slowly, I pulled my phone out and pressed on the walkie-talkie app.

"Ben?"

"Yes?" Ben and Marley answered at the same time.

"I'm in the tunnels. With Benji."

"Oh, God."

DAY FOUR

The Beginning

I tried to remember every movie I'd ever seen. It wasn't better to run, right? Running was bad. Running engaged their prey drive and they'd give chase. Staying still would work, right? Maybe he couldn't see me if I didn't move.

Fuck, that was *Jurassic Park* again.

I slowly turned around with my axe, hefting it in my hands. Benji was walking on scorched paws, with fence marks burned into his face. He was half-way down the tunnel, stumbling toward me pretty quickly for a burned zombie tiger.

I began to slide toward the door that led to Marley's herpetology offices. I could hear her shoo-ing the children into the nursery, heard the door shut. The sound of her fumbling with the keypad to open the door to the tunnels made Benji's head shoot up, staring at the door.

It was better than seeing his dead eyes gazing directly at me.

He'd covered about half the distance in his slow, stumbling gait, and was approximately 10 feet away from me. It was the closest I'd ever been to one of the big cats without heavy-duty protection between us. Part of me marveled at the sheer beauty of him; it was devastating to see the burn marks, to see this magnificent creature staggering on broken and bleeding skin. He was leaving large footprints behind him with every step.

Everything in me screamed that I needed to run—and that I needed to help him. He looked so confused, as if he couldn't figure out where he was and why he was there. My heart broke for him. Maybe I could lead him back to the quarantine section. He clearly didn't know what he was doing. I took a step toward him, reaching out my hand.

The door opened slowly behind me. "What the hell are you doing?" Marley hissed.

"He needs help," I explained quietly. "He doesn't understand."

"He's a giant fucking tiger that wants to eat you, remember? Get in here, now!"

My gut clenched as I realized something else

about this virus—it was hypnotic. The moment I looked away from Benji, the spell broke, and terror came rushing back to greet me. Benji was six feet away and closing.

I began to walk backward, step by step. Falling would not be advantageous at this current moment in time. I could barely breathe. The clouds over his eyes did nothing to hide the malice; once I was no longer entranced, I heard the low, moaning growl rushing over his teeth, over and over again. He settled back on his haunches, getting ready to pounce.

I hit the door and Marley grabbed me by the shirt, hauling me inside. She slammed the door shut just as I heard Benji slam into it. All of the doors at the zoo had the extra protection of metal inside of them . . . but as I saw a paw print warp the center of the door, I realized that we'd never planned for this.

No one could have ever planned for this.

"We've gotta move," I said, turning to Marley. "We can't be here. He's coming in."

"He's not coming in," she soothed me—and shrieked as he slammed into the door again, denting it further.

"He's coming in," I shrieked, and then I heard the children begin to cry.

It whipped Benji into a frenzy. I could hear him snarling and charging the door from the other side as Marley and I began to grab kids and push them through the door to the offices. Marley was in the nursery, making sure that no one was left when I saw it.

"Marley?" I whispered.

"Yeah?" she said, closing all of the doors she could between us and Benji. She came out into the aquarium office, counting the children on her fingers. "We're missing two."

"No we're not!" I yelled over my shoulder as I launched myself into the corner of the room. Hank was standing on top of my desk, hissing and spitting, growling as loudly as his poor little body could. He was standing over the two children that Marley hadn't been able to find.

"Get the kids out of here!" I screamed.

One of the children had eaten the chicken.

Blood couldn't be that color. It was darker than I expected as it pooled beneath the body of one of the children. He hadn't even had a chance to yell; the little girl attacking him must have clamped down on his throat first thing. She tore into his flesh, ripping apart vocal cords and trachea, moaning and making a strange clicking noise with her tongue. She went back to him over and over again, peeling pieces of flesh off of his face gleefully, and I saw his chest rise and fall.

He was still alive.

Marley swallowed hard, staring at the child for a long moment as I tried to pull the girl off of him. Her voice shook as she hollered, "Everyone follow me! It's okay, we've got a plan!" over the crying children.

"The tiger's going to get us!"

"Why is this happening?"

"What's going on?"

"What's wrong with Clarissa?"

"Why is David lying down?"

"I CAN HEAR THE TIGER!"

"Everybody hold hands and make a line. We're going to get out of here right now. Follow me," Marley urged, beginning to lead the children past David's body. I was holding Clarissa by the waist as she clawed and snarled, trying to get back to David. My eyes were everywhere but on him; I could see the shining bone of his spine if I looked closely enough.

The last child finally filed out of the aquarium and I threw Clarissa back at David. "Sorry, David," I whispered, knowing that he was effectively already gone. His small body lay prone on the floor, exposed and devastated, and bile rose up from the depths of my stomach to coat my mouth. I grabbed Hank and ran, listening to the sounds of her rending him apart, piece by piece, as I stopped and locked the door behind me.

#

I threw Marley into explaining the herbivore exhibits near the aquarium; those, at least, we hadn't had to keep in quarantine. Instead of talking about my passion for herd animals, I found myself in the bathroom, locked in a stall, sitting on the floor with my phone in my hands.

"Ben," I said softly, tears streaming down my face. "Ben, where are you?"

"I'm gonna turn mine off for about ten minutes so the kids don't hear you discuss this," Marley advised. I was thankful for her discretion and tact; it was pretty obvious to everyone that I wasn't fit company for children at the moment.

I would never unsee what I saw.

I knew she was still in there, tearing David to shreds. Was this what was going to happen? Were we really going to be overrun by zombie children and animals? My mind was whirling with the possibilities; could any of us really kill a child, no matter how sick he or she might be?

"Little busy Lens," I got back from Ben.

"This is important. One of the kids started to eat another kid."

A long pause. "So it's started?"

"It's started," I said.

"We called the parents and I found the key code in Marley's desk. We've corralled the kids into the infirmary and Dr. Warner is strapping the violent ones down to the stretchers. I don't know what else to do, Lens. I don't know what to do when the parents get here."

"At least we're not trapped in the zoo," I offered hopefully.

"Lenny and Carl are loose at the entrance of the zoo. We're trapped, Lens. Benji's in the tunnels, Lenny and Carl are in the outer ring, and I've got about sixteen kids and three volunteers that might end up like your kid. You can't get out past us."

"That only leaves the loading dock," I said quietly, resting my head against the stall wall.

"I'm going to text you the key code. I've gotta go. One of the kids broke the restraints. I love you."

"I love you too," I said, but he was already gone.

I closed my eyes and took a breath. Marley and I were alone. The children were safe—for the time being, anyway; as long as we stayed near the aquarium and didn't go toward the infirmary. The problem was that the loading dock was on the other side of the zoo, halfway between the aquarium and the front door.

In the tunnels where Benji was.

One of us would have to find a way out. I looked at

my phone, hoping for answers, and found an email from David:

Things are getting bad quickly. There's reports of attacks all over the city. They shut down all the airports and bus stations but I'm afraid it might be too late. I locked myself in the lab and am working on the CDC samples now.

A girl from my Bio 101 class is at the door. She's head-butting the glass. I don't know how much longer it will hold.

Be safe.

-David

It had finally happened. The virus had reached the general populace and was beginning to make people violent. It wasn't just the zoo, and we couldn't blame it on the flu any longer—this was the beginning of the end, unless David—or one of his colleagues—could stop it.

I could almost feel the shifting into my new reality. We passed the empty bear exhibit to watch the gazelles grazing, and my heart clenched. I might never see Africa now, if the government didn't get a hold of the situation fairly quickly.

There might not be an Africa to go to.

My phone dinged me out of my reverie.

Lens—

Went to visit Jeff to discuss findings. Hospital is

gone. They used the same distributor for cafeteria food. I couldn't even get past the lobby before I saw someone acting strangely. There was a sign on the nurse's station not to go up to the patient floors.

Jeff is gone.

I'm working on a vaccine, but with so many already sick . . .

Check the news.

—David

I scrolled over to CNN and my heart dropped.

□□ Headline News □ Levonn Manufacturers Continue to Deny Tainted Chicken □ Attacks Reported Across the Country □ Stay Inside to Await Government Orders □ Military Evacuation Called for NYC, San Francisco□□

At least someone had figured out the cause of this besides us. They knew, and the government could shut them down. Maybe it wasn't too late. Maybe we could get a hold of this thing after all.

"Lens!" Ben shouted over the walkie talkie. I could hear sounds in the background that I couldn't—didn't want to—identify.

"What's wrong?"

"Get them out. Get them all out now."

"Ben—"

"It's . . . I can't describe it. I'm hiding in the bathroom in the infirmary with the door locked. The kids . . ." He choked. "The kids attacked the parents. Get your kids out now! I don't know how long the infirmary door can hold them."

"But what about you?"

"I'll figure something out! Just go!"

I swallowed what felt like shards of glass, whispered "I love you" into the walkie talkie, and turned to walk toward Marley. "Ben thinks we need to get out of here, now. He's not sure how long the door to the infirmary will last, and the kids are . . . well, they're attacking people."

"But how? If they smell our kids coming past to get to the exit . . ." She looked away at the peaceful zebras. "How could this all go so wrong?"

"I don't know, but we've got to make it to the loading dock. It's the only other exit that isn't blocked by rabid children and tigers."

As we planned our exodus, I began to hear noises. Noises that I'd heard before. Noises that happened when we gave Teddy (Ruxpin; some of us liked old 80's toys) a bloodsicle: a bucket-sized cube of frozen water and blood from the butcher's.

I could faintly hear these sounds from behind his exhibit—and I hoped his neighbor hadn't met a terrible fate. I thanked God and Bob Ross that except for the weird fluke with Benji, the quarantines seemed to be holding.

My attention shifted as I heard one of the parents screeching. One of our crows had broken through the mesh in his habitat, and his friends were making a bid for freedom. Freedom—and food.

The crow was tangled in her auburn curls, flapping and pecking at her head. I saw blood as it began to run down her face and took the sobbing child next to her, holding him hard against my chest. "Run!" I yelled as the crows began swooping and diving. It was an incredible stroke of luck that the crows were infected—their aim was off as they dove, hitting the concrete or fences more often than they hit a human. We might have had a chance.

I turned with the child in my arms and looked back to see talons clawing at ruined eye sockets, sticky with a thick goo that I didn't want to contemplate too hard. Swallowing bile, I ran for the doors to the aquarium—and found the group stuffed into the vestibule.

I set down the little boy and he clutched at my leg, sobbing for his mommy. I wished that I had time to make a pretty excuse to help him through this, but I suddenly remembered why we'd evacuated the aquarium in the first place. The little girl who had eaten David now had fingernail marks gouged in her skin, and a perfect "o" of blood ringed around her lips. She was throwing herself at the locked double doors, over and over again, hissing at the children behind it.

I turned and looked behind us. The first of Ben's infected kids was slowly stumbling down the path. The crows were perched on the bar of the aquarium vestibule door, pecking insistently at the glass as low-pitched, broken squawks escaped their beaks.

I turned and looked out the door behind us. The first of Ben's kids was slowly stumbling down the cobbled path. The crows were perched on the bar to open the door, pecking insistently as low-pitched, warbling squawks escaped their beaks. We were trapped.

The truth had come out—the remaining parents were teary-eyed and furious as they looked from one zombie little girl to five zombie crows. The children wailed, overlapping each other as they screamed and begged for answers, and the noise penetrated my brain. It was so hard to think. There was just too much, and a low, almost electrical-sounding buzzing noise filled my brain. I felt myself start to hyperventilate until Marley whistled shrilly.

"Look—I don't fully know what's going on, but it's pretty obvious at this point that there's a mix of super-flu and something else going on here. It seems to create, for lack of a better term, zombie-like behavior." The parents raised their voices again and she yelled over them. "I know this isn't the greatest situation—"

"I know this isn't a great situation, but we—"

That was an understatement. I tuned her out and looked up, away from the little boy screaming into my leg and the parents arguing furiously with Marley. There had to be a way out. The crows and the coordinator, Mrs. LeDoux, were taking turns bashing the door down behind us, and Clarissa was beginning to spiderweb the glass in front. I clenched my fists and reached for my phone to call Ben one last time.

My eyes focused as my attention shifted, and I saw it. "The air vents," I whispered.

Marley was trying to wedge herself behind me to try and get away from the mother that seemed determined to rip her hair out. "What?"

I cleared my throat and held up three fingers, praying my Girl Scout background was close enough to Explorers to count.

One by one, each child spotted me, or one of their fellow explorers, and began to hold up their own three fingers. As the children stifled their sobs and began to find their Explorer-induced bravery, the parents began to look around sheepishly and hold up fingers of their own. It was evident that everyone was terrified—but it was easy for training to take over when someone else took charge of the situation.

“Thank you,” I said softly into the silence. I could hear hitched and painful breathing over the sounds of Clarissa and the others pounding at the doors. “I think I’ve found a way out of here.” I held up my fingers higher as the parents began to talk over each other again, criticizing a plan that they hadn’t even heard yet.

“We’re going to open up the air vent on the ceiling and crawl through the ducts to the loading docks. We’ll be safe up there; there’s no way for the animals or the infected children and adults to climb up. It’s probably cramped and dirty, but it’s safe. I think the boss’ office is on the way, and I can jump down and get the key from his office directly so that we can get out of here.”

Marley nodded in encouragement. “She’s right. I’m going to climb up first – three or four children per one parent behind them, and then Lens is going to take up the back. We can do this, guys. It’s just a little setback, but we’re almost home free.”

Jinx.

Day Four

The Escape

The lone father of the group hoisted Marley up on his shoulders so that she could pry the air vent cover off with his pocket knife. My walkie-talkie app beeped, and I held it close. “Ben?”

“Lens,” he whispered. He sounded out of breath. “The kids broke the glass. They’re all over the zoo now. I can’t stop them. Dr. Warner . . . he’s gone, Lens. Get out. Please. I’m going to try to get out the back window and climb the fence around the zoo. I’ll meet you by the loading dock if I can. I love you.”

I prayed fervently that it wasn’t the last words I’d ever hear him say. Tears trickled freely down my cheeks as I hoisted children into the air, three for every parent volunteer the father pushed up into the ductwork. I realized then, as the father and I stood alone in the foyer, that we had a problem.

"Well, you can't lift me," he said gruffly and grabbed me around the waist. I flailed wildly, rising into the air until I could catch hold of the ceiling. Scrambling, I used his shoulders to lift myself up into the ductwork, and peered down at him from inside.

"How do we get you up?" I asked.

He smiled grimly. He must have been extraordinarily attractive once; he looked like Harrison Ford, but worn, tired and dirty. I could see the heartbreak in his eyes before he opened his mouth. "My daughter's out there," he said simply. "I'm going to go find her."

"You can't! You'll be eaten alive!"

"That's the chance I have to take," he replied. "I can't leave without knowing what happened to her. And if something did happen, then I'm going to stay with her until the end."

Before I could say a word he took a deep breath, turned toward the exit doors, and rammed his body into one of them. The force of his charging rammed the door into Mrs. LeDoux, who fell to the ground, groaning and screeching. He jumped over her prone body as the boy began to give chase, and started running toward the infirmary.

"Good luck," I whispered. I could see the crows flying slowly after him, flapping wildly, uncoordinated but angry. I could only hope that he found his daughter before the crows found him.

I exhaled slowly and looked ahead at the children in front of me. "Let's go," Marley said, her voice echoing quietly through the ducts. I heard a chorus of "Ew"'s and "It's so dirty!"'s and almost laughed as I sat tearfully at the beginning of the airway. After a moment of getting myself together and praying for that brave man, I began to crawl.

"Don't look down!" Marley hissed. "Everybody look straight ahead. Pay attention to where you're going. There's lots of ways you can get lost and . . ."

Her voice echoed and bounced through the metal ducts and I lost the gist of what she was saying—but I knew it was a lie. Every ten feet or so there was another grate that I could see through—and I felt more than heard Marley shushing the kids.

Benji was down there, feasting on a badger. Its stomach was torn open, intestines laying like dropped toothpicks strewn across the floor. His face was deeply embedded in the badger's body, and horrible sucking and chomping noises echoed through the tunnels.

"Don't scream!" Marley shushed them. "If you scream, they might find us."

It wasn't the most diplomatic way to shut the kids up, but with a few small whimpers, we continued on past Benji. I stopped above him, staring down at the beauty of his coat and the sadness of his blank, dead eyes. I loved all of Ben's cats, and seeing him lift up his head, heart in mouth with blood dripping onto his scorched, electrocuted paws drove bile from my stomach to my lips. I swallowed firmly, gagging on the taste, and tried to control my breathing.

Benji looked up.

I held my breath, shivering as I stayed as still as I could. I could hear the children knocking around as they crawled; it echoed through the concrete tunnels, and it seemed as loud as a bomb going off. My chest began to burn as Benji scented the air, and finally went back to his badger.

I saw a tail a few feet behind him. Badgers, then.

I tried to make as little noise as possible as I crawled through the ducts. It was a bloodbath—I could hear the kids whimpering, the parents shushing in their own strained voices, and Marley grimly leading them ahead of me. I could see bars ripped apart, prey animals strewn all over their inside habitats and the tunnels. A lone cheetah was ripping into what was left of a young hippopotamus; I didn't even want to speculate how that had happened. The level of carnage was terrifying. If this was happening in the zoo, what was happening outside?

I didn't have long to wonder.

As we passed the feeding/medical prep area and peeked in on Bacon, who was thankfully silent, the line stopped. I was sitting in the air duct, just in front of the divide between prep and the tunnels, when it happened.

It was a small creaking sound, one that I overlooked. It was the sound of metal on metal, of rusted screws losing their grip, the feeling of a small earthquake and then a jarring bowing in the metal. I watched in horror as two children, a boy and a girl, struggled to move forward only to fall through the rusted metal grating over the habitat tunnels.

They sat on the concrete floor, dazed, staring up at the duct from which they fell, and I closed my eyes briefly. We were far enough away that Benji and the cheetah wouldn't be a problem, thankfully. But it did mean that someone had to boost them back up—or lead them through the tunnels.

A loud creak was our only warning as two feet of the air ducts fell through the ceiling, dangling at an angle toward the floor. I could hear Marley swearing, and the mother that had been in front of me shouted "Is everyone okay? Emma!"

Emma and Jace sat on the concrete, looking up

tearfully. There was no longer a way for me to cross the gap—and only one option through that I could see.

"Keep going!" I called to Marley. And then I jumped.

It was more of a graceless fall than a jump, but I still got to the ground uninjured. Emma stood protectively over the sandy-haired boy, holding a large flashlight like a club and looking fully capable of beating the hell out of zombie badgers. She looked up as we heard the small bumps and exclamations as the group moved past us through the ducts.

I watched, bemused, as the girl who couldn't be more than ten years old straightened up and threw her shoulders back. "Let's go," she stated, with authority. "Ms. Eleanor, how do we get to the door we need?"

I hid a small smile. I had a feeling that this little girl was used to taking charge. "We follow the tunnel for a while first," I explained as we began to follow Marley's and the other children's journey. Emma held Jace's hand, firmly leading him down the tunnel. Maybe it wouldn't be such a disaster, I thought.

That was when we found out what the noises we'd heard outside had been. Because of course we did.

The problem with the maintenance tunnels and habitat spaces was that in an emergency, the gates to the habitats were locked down—but it seemed as if this emergency had hit before most of the gates could close. This meant that any animal determined enough could, theoretically, break out of the floor-to-ceiling steel cages reinforced on three sides with concrete. We'd already seen what Benji and Sahala had been willing to do to get to the uninfected—it was no longer a warning in the manual, or a vague possibility.

Jace shrieked—a long, high-pitched sound that echoed through the hall. I stopped and stared with Emma at the badgers on the ground.

At least, I thought they had once been badgers.

I saw a fluff of something that may have started life as a tail, and my heart broke at the small, striped nose. The rest of its fur fell to the wayside, bones splintered and rent apart with no regard for life or limb. Jace buried his face in his hands. The blood on the concrete walls were stained higher than he was tall.

I counted enough parts to guess that whoever had gotten to the badgers had killed at least five of them. Emma's face was pale. "What did THAT?" she whispered.

She seemed to be handling it better than myself or Jace, who promptly threw up what looked like hot dogs all down the front of his shirt. At least, I hoped that it had been hot dogs. There wasn't an ounce of maternal instinct in me enough to get close enough to check—or help.

I exhaled slowly, placing my hand on the blood-stained concrete for balance. I felt the heel of my shoe rocking slightly and grimaced as I stepped off a thick badger's tooth. Emma's question was a good one—what *had* done this?

Jace's face was so pale that I missed the warning signs. I turned to Emma and sighed. "I don't know, kiddo," I replied. This day needed to end before another disaster showed itself. I held my hands out for the kids, intent on making our way down the tunnel—it was the only excuse I had to explain why I didn't notice until Jace slowly raised a shaking hand to point behind me.

Something within me told me to stay still. I felt myself beginning to shake as Jace and Emma began to back away. I turned my head as little as possible until I caught it with my peripheral vision.

Of course it was Teddy, the half-ton brown bear that one of the other keepers, not Ben and myself, had quarantined.

He was almost close enough to make sure that we couldn't escape—and while I knew it was fear, not reality, I almost felt the hot, wet breath drenched in the scent of blood tingle across the back of my neck. He wasn't that close—yet. I took a breath.

"Don't run," I said softly. My voice was even, not panicked, and I almost felt a surge of pride for finding one motherly instinct in me.

Teddy moaned, and a shiver licked down my spine. I heard his claws click against the floor as he took another step toward me. My eyes darted around the hallway, looking for somewhere, anywhere to escape to. I saw the gate for the gazelle habitat, and a surge of excitement flowed through me. As I opened my mouth to signal to the kids to press the gate release, Jace lost what little nerve he had left.

He screamed, and Emma froze, pushing herself into the concrete wall as if to be absorbed by it. Teddy blinked slowly and half-turned at the echo that Jace had created, and for a single moment I began to relax. He would surely turn and go the other way.

And then Jace began to run.

"Hit the red button, Emma!" I hissed ,and stood in the middle of the walkway, spreading out my arms and legs. Time to see if "make yourself big" really worked.

It was then that I saw two problems—Jace was still running, with Teddy gearing up to follow, and Emma's tiny hand couldn't reach to release the gate button.

Teddy dropped to all fours and stared Jace in the eye.

Day Four

Is it Bedtime?

My life began to run in stop-gap pictures—one flash, and then another. I saw Teddy closing in on Jace. I saw him trip on his shoelaces. I saw Emma gasp and scream as I slowly backed up toward the red button.

I saw Jace die.

Teddy roared, his voice shaking the very ground, and he buried his face in Jace's soft belly as he lay struggling on the floor. The screams were inhuman—wolf howls of agony and fear as blood rained down like errant sparks from a firework.

I heard his small voice hiccuping, slowing, as I grabbed Emma and buried her head against my chest. She shook, eyes wide open and unseeing. Tears rolled down both of our faces as we stood silent in the aftermath of the virus' rage. It took forever and it only took a moment for the sounds to wither from screams to Teddy's growls and moans—and a slick, wet flesh sound as it was torn and consumed.

I groped the wall for the button to the gazelle habitat and fell into it with Emma in my arms. I ushered her out of the indoor habitat and into their "plains," sinking down into the long grasses before either of us saw more that we'd never be able to forget.

Emma sat quietly beside me, staring into a blade of grass, and whispered: "I want my mommy."

My heart clenched. She was so small and so brave and I wanted nothing more than to deliver her mommy right then and there. "I'm sure she and the others are on the docks by now, safe and sound," I offered hopefully.

She shook her head, dirty-blond hair sticking to the sweat on her face. "She wouldn't come," she said simply. "She stayed at the food place and wouldn't come talk to me or anything."

Emma sobbed once before covering her eyes and mouth with her hands. It made my skin crawl to think of what her life must be like that she cried so silently.

"I'm sorry," I said uselessly. I paused, wondering how much a child should really know about what was going on. "Did you hear from mommy or your teachers that there's a big flu, a bad sickness that a lot of people are getting?"

She nodded ,resting her head on my knee. "Mommy said granny has it and we can't go see her 'cause the hospital is full of sick people," she said.

"I think your mommy and some of the others caught the sickness, too," I said carefully. "It makes people feel so sick that it's really hard to talk or walk around." I figured 'and cannibalism' probably wasn't information that she would need to know.

"Is that why the bear was mean?"

Man, she was bright! It took several Phds and college-educated zookeepers to figure out what she intuited in mere moments—that the sicknesses were connected. I nodded slowly. "Sometimes, sickness that people have acts differently in animals. That's why we're out here, where it's safe—the gazelles aren't sick." I mostly lied, pointing to the herd that was near the fence—at least it was true that they'd never eaten chicken in their lives.

My phone beeped loudly and I almost dropped it in my haste to shut it up. My video chat window popped up as I answered, showing David's pale, anxious face, with his office in the background.

"Oh, thank God, Lens," he breathed in a rush. "I had to lock myself in my office. It's bad out here, Lens."

He took his phone and aimed it out the window of his office. I counted five infected people at the door, fists banging against the wood slowly. David panned to the window overlooking the parking lot and I gasped.

Cars were overturned, windows broken. The shops across the street were covered in shattered glass and trash, remnants of looting. A street sign was bent and twisted, but worst of all was the crowd.

It was obvious that various students and faculty had tried to corral the herd of infected in the courtyard. Desks, dressers and even a couch or two barricaded every exit, and I counted at least 30 people standing in the same direction, staring beyond the barricade, obviously victims of the sickness.

He lifted and angled his phone and tears sprung to my eyes. I'd gone to the same school through my bachelor's, Master's, and now doctorate. To say I was attached to this little school was an understatement. My heart broke to see that their quarantine hadn't worked, either.

Dark pools of blood stained the brick walkways, along with the bodies. Students and teachers of all ages lay strewn on the ground like so much trash, their bodies only shells and casings to those who lusted after their insides. Doors were pounded through, broken and bashed in by the infected who hadn't felt the pain they'd inflicted upon themselves.

I swallowed hard, realizing that it was only a matter of time before they learned to climb the stairs. David was running out of time.

"It spread like wildfire, Lens," he said heavily. "The infirmary was overrun this afternoon and it went downhill from there." A defeated chuckle crackled through the phone. "We can't cure it. At least, I can't, and at last report, one third of the CDC staff in Atlanta was dead. It's over, Lens. Stay at the zoo, at least you'll be safe behind the gates.

I looked at the screen incredulously. "Jeff's gone. Ben is MIA, and so is Dr. Warner. Marley led a group of Explorers and their parents through the air vents to the loading docks, running from a tiger, and we just escaped a frigging zombie bear that ate a small child. We're anything but safe, David. If anything, this was practically ground zero."

David closed his eyes slowly. "The White House stopped making announcements two hours ago. I'm going to try to head for the roof. There have been helicopters circling the campus. If I get rescued, I'm coming for all of you."

I smiled weakly, knowing that our chances were slim of David ever coming to be our Knight in Doctoral Armor. "Be safe," I offered, in vain.

The world was ending, and I was sitting in a field of gazelles with a small child for company. I leaned down and kissed the top of her head, watching the gazelles graze peacefully. If only we could stay, just like this.

#

Of course it didn't stay that way.

I smelled it before I saw it—the now-familiar scent of scorched fur and flesh. I stilled in the tall grass as the gazelles' ears perked up. I held a finger to Emma's lips and she nodded, eyes wide. I was running out of predators that I knew about. I wished I'd spent more time talking to Ben about his damn cats and canids. I needn't have worried about my lack of knowledge, though; from the scent, it had to be one of the cats—the only ones with electric fences.

I covered Emma's ears as I heard a scream that sent a chill down my spine. The older gazelle that I called "Blue" was dying; I could see him struggling through the blades of grass as I felt more than heard the beginnings of a stampede.

The problem with a zoo stampede is that no matter how great your prairie habitat is, eventually there's some kind of fence to run into. More importantly, it was a fence that was high enough—or with the ground sunken low enough—that the herd couldn't jump it.

I saw the spotted leopard pair before they saw us—crouching awkwardly on the ground, their normal grace overshadowed by the disease growing in every cell. Drool slowly slipped down chipped teeth, sliding through the male's lips and beginning to drip toward the ground. He had been the one to get them out—I didn't want to think of the damage he'd done to himself getting both out of quarantine and through the fence.

I would never forget the image of him panning his head to the side. His right eye was no longer an orb, but a swollen, pink hole that seeped blood and plasma. The claws on his right front foot were burned off at an angle that made me believe that he'd sheared off a toe or two as well. My heart broke to see his mate limping to circle the herd; broken chain-link had snapped off in one of her paw pads.

Through it all, the reason why I wasn't a mother became glaringly obvious—I'd forgotten about Emma. Not only had I forgotten about her, she had disappeared from my world completely until her nerves broke entirely.

She stood up and screamed.

Over and over again, a loud, piercing howl

reverberated across the plains until I dove to tackle her. She hit the ground hard and gasped a startled cry as she tripped over a rock, landing on her arm. I heard the crack—and so did the leopards.

Emma breathed big, heaving sobs as I grabbed her by the waist and held her as tightly as I could, her arm immobilized between us, and even though I knew exactly how bad of an idea it was—I ran.

I ran for the fence to the next habitat over, fairly confident all the badgers were dead. We hit the herd hard, as I tried to maneuver my way into the middle of the gazelle group, hoping the leopards would get distracted.

They didn't.

I heard more than felt it when the female reached me. I could see the chain link fence—it was so close. I saw the herd hit the fence and huddle together against it—and there she was. Her mate was busy with my favorite elderly gazelle, but her golden, opaque gaze met mine and she snarled, reaching for me with teeth.

I had never been more thankful for zombies than I was at that moment. She fell, unbalanced, and it almost hurt to see her struggle to stand, until I saw her claws extend.

I shoved Emma toward the fence and screamed at her to climb. Her protests of pain lasted only moments as she stared in horror at the cats and turned to scramble over the fence one-handed.

Two male gazelles turned and began to come my way. Everything felt like slow motion, my life flipping unsteadily frame-to-frame. I almost felt grateful for the males' defense of me when I heard what I thought were my jeans rip—and in retrospect, that may have been part of it. I felt the bulk of her massive paw impact with my left leg before I felt the searing, blinding sensation that somehow even *tasted* of pain. My leg refused to do its job any longer as I steadfastly avoided looking at my thigh, focusing instead on Emma's trek up the fence.

Two things happened then—I remembered the drop-off between the fence and the badger's habitat that surely Emma could not scale, and I saw the outline of a man jump down from the top of the habitat, heading toward me at a fast clip.

"Get the kid!" I screamed, dragging myself further into the herd. My passage was slicked by blood, and I could feel each individual blade of grass caressing the split and gushing skin of my thigh.

The gazelles reared and kicked as the female crept toward me, snapping her teeth and extending her claws once more. Sunlight glinted off a single claw as I shifted my gaze to my thigh.

The world went red—and then black.

#

I opened my eyes to a fuzzy view of hay and the sound of a sniffling child. It took me a moment to realize that that probably was not what heaven was supposed to look like, so evidently, I was alive. What seemed like miles of veterinary tape was wrapped around Emma's arm, with a metal spatula sticking out by her fingers. Work with what you have, I suppose.

I blinked unsteadily until the fuzziness cleared and stared silently at the sight before me. I flailed wildly, coming up with a pair of wooden tongs, and began smacking the shit out of Ben.

"I! Thought! You! Were! Dead!" I snarled, whapping him with the tongs with each word until I fell into his arms in a heap of sobs. Or, I really fell over against him, seeing as how I was laying on my back with my leg in the air, propped up on a feed bucket. More to the point, I realized that Dr. Warner was alive, well, and using veterinary tools to sew the massive claw marks on my thigh. The needle alone made me want to vomit all over him. As I watched, I wondered what the hell they'd drugged me with to keep me from screaming.

I saw parts of myself that you never think about when you're at the meat counter. White and stringy things, deep red and purple things, and flesh that looked like a wrinkled bald man's head. At least my sense of humor was still intact.

Until the stitches started back up. My sense of humor was directly proportional to the amount of suck that a needle going through your skin equaled. I stared up at Ben, somewhere between menacing and gleeful. "Why aren't you dead?"

Dr. Warner made another knot and interrupted Ben before he could even begin. "Because we're both idiots that don't know what's good for us," he said mildly.

Ben hesitated. "Some of that, yes," he hedged. "Some of it also involved going back to Mary's office to get the shotgun that she duct-taped under her desk in case some day she had to be a hero."

"Beginning. Start from the beginning."

He sighed, resting against the metal bars. I realized we were in the gazelle habitat again and panicked. "Wait, where's Teddy? Where's the leopards?"

Clearing his throat, Ben looked aside at the mound of hay, his mouth working with no sounds coming out. "What he means to say is that we shot them," Dr. Warner said softly. "We found out early on that if you shoot them in the head, it kills whatever's driving the virus."

"Ben can't shoot things. Ben can't shoot a water gun without getting himself wet."

"Ben learned how to shoot things," Ben himself said gravely. "After you left, I climbed out the window of the bathroom in the infirmary and onto the roof. I jumped over to the roof of the gift shop and found Dr. Warner still there, blocked in by the kids at the food court. We went down the back stairs to Mary's office."

"She's still there," Dr. Warner said. "You guys did a good job with the duct tape."

"Duct tape is a big thing at zoos," I murmured, wincing as Dr. Warner began wrapping what little vet tape we had around my leg, securing it with the aforementioned duct tape. "Multipurpose tool. Very useful. What happened next?"

"We raided the tool closet in the gift shop and Indiana Jones'd it across the top of the exhibits," he said, rubbing his eyes. "Luckily, I guess, the cats knocked out the electric fences when they left. Or burned them out. It's hard to tell, and I don't really think I want to know anyway. I learned that if properly motivated I can, in fact, climb a rope."

"Properly motivated?"

"He means we got chased by the killer leopards before they found you," Dr. Warner said, leaning back against the wall with Ben. "It's been largely a matter of who's going to get us first, people or animals."

"Well, my news isn't so great either," I said, sitting up slowly. My head spun and I reached out. Ben braced me immediately, helping me to sit, propping me up against his shoulder. "Zombie crows attacked the parents, we got stuck in the vestibule of the aquarium, and Marley tried to lead us to freedom through the air vents to the loading docks. Somewhere between all of this, I got a call from David, and we're fucked. I mean, we are really, royally fucked. This isn't just the zoo—it's everywhere. They're shutting down major cities, airports, everything. He's hostage at the campus right now, praying they don't figure out how to climb the stairs."

Ben whistled incredulously, closing his eyes. "That was news I didn't really want to hear."

"Well, I didn't mention the zombie kid who ate another kid in the aquarium was the reason we had to go through the air ducts," I muttered. "Zombie crows and your kids on one side, her and her dead friend on the other. Hank and I were making our way nicely at the end of the line when the air ducts gave out and me and two kids fell through." I blinked. "Wait, where's Emma?"

Ben gestured to the top of the hay bale. Emma looked so small up there; her bravery was gone, replaced by a deep sadness that I'd never before seen in a child. She lay quietly, but I knew somehow that she was awake. No one could sleep after what she'd just seen.

"Oh thank God and Bob Ross," I sighed.

"What's with the Bob Ross?" Dr. Warner asked curiously.

"Oh. Marley's an atheist, and I got sick of her snickering every time I said something like 'thank God.' So I decided that we now pray to Bob Ross as well, because he's dead, and he's lovely, and everything in his world is pretty trees, and if we could all have a little of whatever Bob Ross had (imbibed or otherwise), the world would be a better place. So, Bob Ross."

Dr. Warner nodded slowly. "That makes a disturbing amount of sense. However, we can't stay here forever. You said you were heading to the loading dock?"

"Yeah. John's office is on the way, theoretically. I had figured I could bust the air vent above his desk, climb down, find the key, and use his desk to get back up." I stared down at my leg. "Maybe not now."

"Probably not," Ben said. He hesitated, squinting out at the prairie behind the gate. "You said zombie crows?"

"Zombie crows," I confirmed.

"So . . . there's also zombie hawks, seagulls, owls, and pigeons?"

"Probably not pigeons. I don't think I've ever seen them take off with chicken nuggets. But yeah, big friggin' zombie birds."

"And we're still missing the wolves and the chimps."

Dr. Warner nodded. "I haven't seen a wolf since I came in," he said. "But that's an interesting question. Chimps are omnivores; would they eat pieces of chicken?"

Ben shrugged. "That's not my area," he said simply. "I know it's stupid that we don't have overlapping knowledge, but as zookeepers, I had enough to worry about with the cats and canids. I'm more concerned about the wolves. Normally, they want nothing to do with humans other than me—they wouldn't hurt a fly. But now?" He shook his head. "I have a feeling that anywhere near their habitat is going to be a nightmare of epic proportions. Zombies that fight in pack formation? No fucking thank you."

I mentally went through the map in my head of the zoo before sighing, closing my eyes. "We don't really have a choice, do we," I said softly.

"No," a small voice chimed in. It was weak and wavering, but Emma sat up slowly, crossing her arms around her knees and hugging them tightly to her chest. "I don't think we get to have choices anymore. I think we're in really big trouble, and all the animals are going to find us. And I think we're gonna die like my mommy died, because you said zombie, and I know what a zombie is, and we're all going to die." She said this calmly, as if she'd accepted and understood her fate better than any of us had.

The adults in the room stared at each other for a long moment. She'd summed up the situation pretty succinctly; she'd already seen one of her friends die, and she was pretty damn sure at this point that her mom had died, too. Whatever I'd thought about kids before, I knew now that they weren't stupid, and it took all of us a moment to pull ourselves together enough to come up with what to say.

"Well, we're going to do our best not to die," Ben said slowly. "You're right, the animals are going to find us. But we've got a gun, and Dr. Warner is really good with it. He learned how to use a gun shooting darts at animals to make them go to sleep. So he's going to watch out for us while Lens and I figure out how to get out of the zoo."

She looked from one of us to the other, frowning, her fingers in her mouth. With a silent nod she slipped off of her hay bale and joined us on the floor, holding her hand out for Ben's. It seemed as if our foursome was it; we were the zoopocalypse squad, and all I could do was hope we were unstoppable. I wondered how many shells we had left for the shotgun; this could be interesting.

Day Four

The Last Stand (Part One)

One day, there will be a story about the one intelligent being in the universe that doesn't tempt fate by saying the word "interesting" to refer to the future. It's similar to saying "it's so quiet" in the emergency room—an immediate curse, a jinx that would follow you around for the rest of your shift.

That story was not going to be ours, because of course I'd curse us in the middle of what was probably the end of the world as I knew it.

Our apocalypse checklist included one veterinarian who learned how to use a gun by tranquilizing animals and hoping bullets weren't much different; one zookeeper who had watched his entire career turn into zombie animals; one prey-studying PhD student who was beaten up by a tiger; and one traumatized ten-year-old girl with a likely broken arm. If this truly was the end of the world, I would be betting on team zombie zoo, not us.

Dr. Warner had a little hunch (aided by some truly awful sounds) that the leopards were busy with what was left of my gazelle herd. I had no words for the scene before me when we crept to the outside of the habitat; while I was overly familiar with dissection, this was beyond the pale.

Gazelle lay prone on their sides with large claw trails down their chests and bellies. I could see puncture wounds, and even an errant canine tooth sticking out of black, split intestines. Leia and Han, the leopards, were ears-deep in the distended belly of a mother gazelle.

Dr. Warner wordlessly grabbed the rope he and Ben had helpfully tied knots into and caught the loop on a rock near the top of the habitat.

Ben carefully pulled Emma, who hadn't said a word since her little speech, up onto his back. "Don't let go," he warned.

She glanced over at Leia, whose paw was stained by blood. "No," she said. "I won't."

Ben scaled the rope fairly quickly for someone with an injured, semi-drugged child on his back. I learned the hard way that I was not, in fact, cut out for America's Ninja Warrior, as I wobbled up the rope with one leg and two noodle-limp arms. Dr. Warner was forced to jump onto the rope quickly and brace my good leg on his shoulder to help me pull myself up.

Exhausted, I sat down on top of the habitat and listened, really listened. I no longer heard normal animal sounds; no soft chuffing of the cats, the howling of the wolves, the quirky little sounds that crows made. There was a breathtaking silence punctuated by slick, wet sounds, and teeth mashing against bone. I closed my eyes, sighing quietly, before cracking an eye to look at Dr. Warner. "How did you learn how to lasso rocks?"

He raised a brow. "How exactly do you think we catch animals that we've tranquilized?"

I frowned. "Somehow I thought the answer would be more exciting than that." I lay back against the habitat roof, staring up into the darkness of the sky. Stars were abundant; it was beautiful out here at the zoo, with little light pollution and a lot of opportunity to stargaze. It was almost pretty, if you ignored the fact that everything in the zoo was trying to kill us, all at once.

I glanced down at Leia and Han, who had slunk off into the night after their gazelle buffet, and chanced a glance at my cell phone. No word from David or Marley, and I didn't dare call Marley unless

I knew she was in no danger of being eaten. I worried for my friends; somehow, not knowing where they were was worse than knowing exactly what situation I was in at the moment: broken, on a roof, and not sure I had the strength to get out.

"So how do we get out of here?" I asked finally.

Ben sighed. "Luckily, we can get to the top of the tunnels from here. We'll have to use the rope to get over the areas that don't have tunnels, or where the tunnel doesn't have a roof. If Dr. Warner and I can make it from the pharmacy to here, we can surely make it to John's office."

I nodded and slowly stood up, testing the wrapping on my thigh. It seemed to be holding everything together that had been falling apart, but the painkillers were starting to wear off, and it took all of my strength not to collapse in front of Emma. "How are you doing, Emma?"

She shrugged, four fingers in her mouth. "We're all gonna die," she sang with a lisp around her hand. "We just don't know when."

I turned and looked at Dr. Warner, Ben, and back to Emma. I'd never seen a child deal with trauma like this first-hand (obviously); was this normal? Or did the zoo break Emma? Ben took a deep breath and held his hand out for the little girl. "You're right, we're all going to die," he said. "But not today."

We all shared a defiant look before we began to walk—slowly—toward the tunnels and the next habitat. It was killing me to not call my friends, but I had to trust in their abilities to keep themselves safe. Worrying about it wasn't going to help us get off the roof.

As I surveyed the walkway made by the tunnels, I briefed a smile. John's office was only half a zoo away. If all we had to do was walk on top of the tunnels til we got there, we were golden.

#

We weren't golden. The first obstacle came when one of the cats' habitats had a gap between it and the next one for access to the electric fence's panels. While I granted the benefit of the doubt that they somehow couldn't get service equipment into the tunnels to maintain the fences, I had a fervent desire to kick the zoo planners' asses for this. Ben and Dr. Warner—

"Dr. Warner?"

He stopped and turned. "What's wrong? Are you bleeding again? I brought—"

"No," I assured him. "At least, I'm pretty sure I'd have noticed if I was. What's your first name?"

"You stopped us planning our daring escape to ask me to introduce myself?"

I looked for Emma. She was currently playing with dandelions that had begun to grow in cracks of the concrete. Softly, I replied, "There's a pretty decent chance that the kid is psychic and at least one of us is gonna end up dead or a zombie. I think we're on a first-name basis now, don't you?"

"Point taken. Josh. It's Josh." He turned back to Ben without another word.

"Nice to meet you, Josh. Now kindly figure out how the hell we can get from Point 'A' to Point 'B' without becoming Point 'Z.'"

Josh began to toss our rope carefully at a pipe on the roof of the exhibit next to ours. I had decided that I would have to shift my focus from what had lived there to how difficult the makings of their habitats were to continuing my current level of existence. I couldn't think of how many animals were predators vs. prey, how many had been eaten, or how many children and parents we'd lost in the last few hours.

If this chaos was scaled properly and I thought of the towns, cities, metropolitan areas just in a 50-mile radius—it was a disaster. Any domesticated pet who'd been thrown an errant chicken nugget, college students and kindergarten teachers and even toddlers would be affected. Could zombies use guns? Policemen and firemen could be affected. Hell, pilots that were actually CURRENTLY FLYING A

PLANE could be affected. The more I thought about what could and probably had happened, the more I began to shake.

I sat down slowly, putting my head between my knees and taking deep breaths. I could feel the panic rising like an electric shock through my veins, crackling wildly and crashing through me to overwhelm my senses. This wasn't just my zoo or my college—what little family I had left, my friends, the guy who delivered my pizza, and regardless what I thought of him, the president—could be affected. The whole world could be coming down around our ears, and we were stuck in a zoo being hunted by some of the fastest, most tenacious creatures in the world.

Ben crouched down in front of me, peering upside-down between my knees. He was a hell of a contortionist when he had to be. "I'm sorry that we don't have time to talk about this," he said softly. "I wish we did. But as far as I know, we're the last four people in the entire zoo that aren't zombies, and we need to get out of here—or find a way to rob a Wal-Mart and fortify the place after dealing with all the animals. I could handle either one. But I need to know you can keep your shit together."

It sounded much more rude than it was. Ben knew that I was normally a pretty unflappable individual—only massive crowds and claustrophobia plagued me. I was annoyed by fear, and the implication that I could maybe NOT get my shit together galvanized me. I shook off the panic, took a deep breath, and stood up with Ben's help.

"I've got my shit together," I replied.

Emma looked at me curiously. "I know what that word means and I don't think that's how you use it," she said skeptically.

"Look up the word 'colloquialism' in the dictionary if we ever get out of here," I suggested, and grabbed her free hand in mine. We walked over to the sketchy bridge Ben and Josh had made—and by sketchy bridge, I meant Josh was holding a rope that bridged the gap over a massive electrical grid panel and Ben was slowly stepping on it to see if he could hold it.

"What the hell are you doing? That's not going to work! That's not how any of this works!"

Dr. Josh glanced at me, less than amused. "Do you have a better plan?"

"No. But I just wanted to put in my opinion on how bad of an idea this is before I get eaten by zombie deer or something."

"Now you're just playing favorites. I'm pretty sure your herds are gone, Lens." He paused, looking over at me for a long moment. "We have to get across. There's no other way."

I looked over his shoulder to see Han and Leia sitting patiently in front of the facade that we currently sat on top of. They stared with that blank, opaque gaze directly toward us. This virus was patient; it had all the time in the world to infect the rest of us.

I heaved myself over to the rope and held on with Josh. “Let’s get Ben over first,” I offered. “The two of us can hold the rope, then we can send the kid over.”

Josh hesitated, looking at Ben. “Are you sure you can hold it, Lens?”

“Do I have a choice?”

“Love conquers all,” he muttered, and nodded at Ben.

#

Love did not conquer all, but the words ‘oh shit’ seemed to have more of an impact on what we were doing. I braced my one good leg and back against the heating and cooling vent that stuck up from the concrete, curled around it like a python. Josh was in front, braced against the lip of the roof with both feet. Emma looked on with fascination; Ben just looked green.

“This is insane,” Ben muttered, for what felt like the 452nd time. The leopards had moved to underneath the location where we’d lassoed the rope and were having our little meeting. We all knew viscerally what we were risking by doing this.

Including Emma.

I didn't know if she was traumatized or fatalistic—maybe both. But it didn't help that she kept speaking to herself, whispering "We're all gonna be eaten and die."

"Well, it's better than being eaten and staying alive as a zombie!" I snapped.

Ben frowned and turned to me. "She's just a kid," he reminded me softly.

I sighed, adjusting my grip on the rope. "I'm sorry, Emma. I know we're all a little scared and you don't deserve for me to take it out on you."

She sat quietly with her fingers in her mouth, looking down over the ledge at the leopards. The female was coated in the blood from my thigh. "Gonna die," she said around saliva-soaked digits. Spitefully.

Ben was the one to sigh next. "I want to send Emma over first."

"She can't climb over the ledge on the next roof by herself," Josh reminded him. "And we need to make sure this holds before we commit to putting a kid on it."

The rope was tied around the duct I clung to, sure. But it wasn't sturdy, leaving Josh and I necessary in holding it up and over the building's edge. It was as tight and secure as we were going to get it. "Just go, Ben." I paused. "Be safe, okay?"

Ben took a breath and sat down on the ledge. He wrapped his ankles around the rope, testing it lightly, and my heart stopped as he clutched it in his hands and slid off the rim.

The rope snapped tight. Josh and I pulled to take the strain off the vent, which made a nerve-wracking squeal of grinding metal—but it held. I couldn't see Ben's trek across, but I felt every movement he made.

It was agonizing. Every time the rope shifted, the vent did as well. I could feel the shaking metal plates behind my back. The moment stretched on until I felt the smallest amount of slack, the venting quieting its rusted grumbles.

" . . . Josh?"

"Mmm?"

"Are you gonna friggin' tell me if I can let go or if I'm now single?" I hissed.

He peered around the vent, grinning with relief. "Sorry. He's good, he's across—it worked."

My entire body melted into the vent. I realized only then that my thigh was burning; a quick look told me that I was bleeding again under my cut-up jeans. At least they'd preserved me some measure of modesty and made me a half-pants, half-shorts contraption instead of making me walk around in my underwear.

"Emma next."

Josh nodded seriously. I realized that he wasn't as old as I'd thought he was—mid-thirties, maybe. As the sunlight glinted on his somewhat fabulous hair, I had a weird and inappropriate desire to match-make for him. Bad situations brought out the best in me.

I leaned back against the vent again as he explained to Emma how this was going to work. I knew how much easier it would have been for her than for us, if not for the arm situation. I almost envied her; children could do the monkey bars with ease. I, on the other hand, fell flat on my ass after one rung. She looped her elbow around the rope, held a knot with her other hand, and crossed her legs at the knees around the thick strands.

"Ow ow ow!" she whimpered, as softly as she could. The rope barely moved. I risked a glance around the vent and saw her body shaking. It was a miracle she could hold herself up at all, I knew—but it was hard enough for the adults to get across without carrying her like a baby monkey. I knew this would hurt, and my heart broke for her, even as frustrating as she was.

"Don't let go! You can do it!"

"I'm gonna get eaten!" she wailed as she slowly began to pull herself across.

It was like a chant: Josh, Ben and I were her cheerleaders, coaching her not to let go, encouraging her across the gap that looked so much bigger than she was. She, on the other hand, was whispering "Zombie leopards, zombie leopards, zombie leopards" over and over, resolutely staring at the rope and not what was below her.

The rope swung perilously and I saw her legs slip. She scrambled, shrieking as she bore weight on her broken arm. She dangled, her shoelace untied, and I could see the leopards' attention change, focusing laser-sights on her. Emma threw her legs up in the air, slinging them around the rope as if she'd done it a hundred times before. My heart pounded in my chest as she wrapped her legs around it with a death grip and took a long, shuddering breath. "Zombie leopards," she whispered.

The rope swung again as she moved another foot. "Zombie leopards."

She was three-fourths of the way there. Foot by agonizing foot she dragged her body across the rope, whispering to herself, a macabre way of urging herself on. When her feet hit the wall her eyes shot open and she saw Ben reaching out for her from the ledge above. "Zombie leopards?"

"No zombie leopards," he assured her, and pulled her up and into his arms.

That was when we both fell apart. I sat gasping against the vent, listening to her sob across the way, Josh looking anywhere but at either of us. This was a nightmare. Everything about the entire zoo-zombie situation was an absolute fucking nightmare, and I couldn't breathe as I heard the snarling begin below us. Emma had awoken their attention, and it was my turn.

"Zombie leopards," I whispered.

#

It was my turn.

I had balked trusting Ben to give me an underwear drawer at his apartment, but somehow it was comforting to trust him at the other end of the rope. He'd saved me once—I knew he'd do it again.

My problem lay in the fact that I had very little use of my left leg. I couldn't shimmy across monkey-style like Ben and Emma had; at least, not quite as effectively.

"You sure you've got this?" I murmured to Josh.

"I won't let you fall," he promised. "We're all in this together." He patted my shoulder lightly and braced himself for my travels. Ben was at the other side; the pipe his end was wrapped around was pretty sturdy, going down through the concrete and several feet beyond the floor, but one could never be too prepared. I knew he wouldn't trust just the pipe.

I slid onto the ledge and wrapped my right leg around the rope as far away as I could reach, and grasped the knot closest to me with a death grip. I didn't look down as I awkwardly fell into space, hoping I had the strength to catch myself.

It sucked so much.

My sutured leg hung down, throwing me off balance. I clung to the rope with all I had, willing myself to move. I moved by precisely one knot when the leopards scented my blood.

"Zombie leopards," I hissed at Josh.

He blanched. "You may want to haul ass, Lens!" He was shouting, using one foot to kick the ledge, trying to draw their attention away from me. I would have been eternally grateful had it worked.

And it might have worked, truly. Had I not broken a stitch or two.

I heaved myself forward another knot. Each faltering movement as my body tried to find somewhere, anywhere for my leg to cling to sent lightning shuddering down my spine. I wasn't capable of relaxing, of letting it dangle while I shimmied across. I kept reflexively lifting my leg and crying out, rivulets of blood trickling down to pool in my shoe. I could feel it fill around my foot, that strange liquid cold that blood seemed to become the moment oxygen hit it, and I could hear the leopards moaning around their broken jaws and shattered teeth.

I made two more knots. My shoe was slowly sliding off my slick socks, and it almost felt like a relief when it finally fell and hit the male in his battered, empty eye.

He grunted and snapped his teeth shut like a crocodile, shoving the clog down his throat. I could hear more than see when it became stuck; his moans turned to wheezes, then the wheezes faded into nothing. He had stopped breathing, yet he still met my gaze with cloudy eyes when I risked a glance.

"Oh shit, they really are zombies," I choked.

The sight of the female clumsily crouching in the grass, flat and silent, gave me incentive to stay moving. My chest was burning almost as much as my leg was; I couldn't even talk about what my noodle-like arms were feeling. "Gotta find a gym," I gasped as I made another knot. "Zombie leopards." Another knot. "Fucking zombie leopards making me go to the gym!"

Somehow, the cursing helped. I made steady progress, gasping and swearing, dripping a line of blood across the gap. As I felt my foot hit the building I sobbed in relief, seeing Ben's face above me.

Of course, that was when the female leapt.

Ben was encouraging me to drop my legs, to come closer on the rope with just my arms and let him pick me up from there; it seemed like a good idea in theory, but the practice was a little difficult when I heard bone hitting concrete.

I shrieked, scrambling to get my bad leg up onto the rope, looking at the dark, almost black blood spattered against the wall. She regrouped, crouching low against the grass, sitting patiently as they both watched me struggle.

"Get me over this stupid wall!" I hissed.

"You have to drop your legs," Ben whispered. "Hurry. Please, Lens, just drop your legs and I'll grab you, I promise!"

A sob escaped my lips as I felt their gaze steadied on my back. "I can't."

"You have to!"

I saw Emma crawl up onto the ledge out of the corner of my eye. "You can do it, Lens," she said softly.

Josh began shouting again from the other side. "You can do it, Lens! Come on!" He kicked the ledge as hard as he could. I suddenly wished we'd all invested in cleats or tap shoes. Something, anything to make more noise, to draw the leopards away from my dripping leg.

I dropped my legs.

Reaching the last few knots drove me to nausea, my body straining with years of sitting behind computers and microscopes and not exercising since I was required to do the Presidential gym test. I wasn't even sure I could have done this when I was a child, let alone a hundred pounds of marshmallow lattes later. It seemed like an eternity before Ben leaned over and grasped my wrists.

I used my good leg to push against the wall, trying to find a grip to pull myself up as best as I could. Ben maneuvered me so that I was draped half over the ledge and could assist myself, and I felt the breeze on my bloody sock as one of the leopards jumped toward me, swatting with massive paws.

I fell onto the roof, panting raggedly. I could feel the blood in my veins, the blood dripping out of my veins, the blood everywhere rushing through my body and decorating the gravel beneath me. "I am never doing that again," I gasped.

Ben squinted, looking at me falling apart on the floor, and then turning around to examine our route. "Well, luckily, the rest of the cats are on the other side of the zoo," he observed. "So hopefully we won't have to."

“You’re an ass, and if we have to do it again, I’m staying on the roof.”

“Fair,” he acknowledged. “I’ll send the zombie bear to come get you.”

We grinned at each other, something like relief spreading through us. I felt guilty when Josh cleared his throat loudly, raising a brow. “This is the hard part,” he reminded us.

Ah, crap.

#

The hard part involved the fact that there was an aging, rusted vent holding Josh’s side of the rope and pretty much hopes and dreams aside from that. He was a slender guy, but muscular from years of heaving unconscious, large animals around for various procedures. I couldn’t remember why the hell we’d thought this was a good idea, except for one: chivalry.

I had an unsettling feeling that Ben and Josh had made a Manly Pact to get The Woman and Child out safely, no matter what. I felt dizzy, and I wasn’t sure if it was blood loss or premonition, but suddenly I had a bad feeling about this. “There’s got to be another way.”

Ben smiled thinly. “There really isn’t,” he said

quietly. "He knew what the cost was when he volunteered to do it this way. It makes sense—I can lift you and Emma, and . . ."

"And he wanted us to stick together."

"How about we not talk about him in the past tense?"

My lips thinned and I turned away, closing my eyes. "I'm scared, Ben."

A tiny hand crept onto my shoulder, and a small Mickey Mouse band-aid was proffered. "I found this in my Explorers kit," she said, gesturing to the little fanny pack I hadn't noticed. "I thought it might help." She paused, looking down at my leg, which was thankfully covered by the vet wrap . . . though the blood was pretty evident in a swathe down my calf. "It can't hurt?" she tried, obviously mimicking something she'd heard her mother say.

My heart lurched. Emma was trying so hard to be brave after she'd lost herself with the leopards—I wanted nothing more than to hold her close and keep her safe from this new reality, but I knew I couldn't. "Thank you," I said quietly, taking the band-aid. "It helps a lot."

She smiled shyly and gestured to Ben. "He has an Explorers kit too," she said. "Maybe he has more band-aids."

I frowned, turning, and saw that Ben did indeed

have an overloaded fanny pack. "Please remind me to make fun of you at a later date when it's appropriate for wearing a fanny pack," I said.

"I will," he replied mock-gravely, before reaching into the aforementioned sign of dork-hood and grabbing some more vet tape and butterfly sutures. "How about the two of you work on Lens' leg while Josh and I worry about getting him over? You can sit over there on the other vent and watch for help."

Emma nodded brightly, taking the tape and sutures and my hand as well. "Let's go, Lens. I have my badge for first aid, I can help."

I bit my lip and saluted Josh across the wall. Ben had thankfully pointed out a place where I could watch, and if Emma sat on the roof, she wouldn't be able to see. I sat down on the vent and slowly began to unwrap my leg, praying it was just two or three sutures instead of a handful.

Emma took a small bottle of hand sanitizer, clearly not understanding the repercussions of putting alcohol on an open wound—though, really, she had the right idea—and began doctoring my leg, beginning with cleaning the blood off of my foot with her package of tissues. She took off my squishy sock, making a face, and tossed it onto the roof. "I don't think we can save the sock," she said seriously.

Josh gingerly climbed onto the rope, hanging as

lightly as he could. He moved slowly but with efficiency, without flailing the way that I had. In little time, he was a third of the way across, and Emma had begun mopping up above my knee.

"You bleed a lot," she observed, wiping everywhere but the sutures and the three split stitches. I appreciated the concern, actually; she was a pretty good little nurse. It was almost as if she knew the more blood was on me, the more likely we were to draw attention.

Josh had *my* attention. He adjusted his grip, taking a breath so deep that I could see it, and continued on toward the halfway point. I strained to listen for the leopards past Emma's chattering and heard only their moans, not the chuffing sound they liked to make before pouncing. I began to relax.

I would forever blame myself for what happened next.

Day Four

The Last Stand (Part Two)

I had no warning. There was no "Hold your breath, Lens!" or "This is gonna hurt, Lens!" There was a little girl mopping blood off of my thigh and unwrapping my wound, and then there was a little girl dumping a quarter of a cup of hand sanitizer into a deep, open wound.

I screamed.

I screamed, and Josh jumped. Josh jumped, and the rope went taught, straining against the pipe and the vent. The rope strained, and I could hear the strands slowly unwinding, creaking, cracking.

Josh was halfway across the gap when the vent collapsed.

I ran, half-doctored but thankfully no longer bleeding as Ben struggled to pull the rope as hard as he could. Muscles heaved with exertion as he grunted, hauling hand over hand in slow motion, as Josh tried to scramble up the rope and over the wall. It was easier to climb vertically, thank God, and his hand reached for the top of the ledge when she launched off of her strong haunches and flew through the air.

Her teeth were still sharp enough to wrap around his calf.

I heard his breath catch in his throat, a tiny hitch and gulp of air, as the weight of the leopard slowly began to tear the muscle off of the back of his leg. She dropped to the ground, wrestling with the chunk of muscle, and her mate circled around her, pacing back and forth, waiting.

Josh's fingertips reached for Ben as I dove for Ben's feet, pushing my full weight onto them, holding him down so he could reach farther.

He was gasping, air passing through his lips rapidly, his eyes dilated with pain. He touched Ben's hand just for a moment, skin to skin, and I almost sobbed with relief that it was almost over.

The leopard struck.

He jumped higher than his mate, catching Josh's belt, digging his teeth hard into it and hanging. The weight of the leopard pulled hard; it was a dead weight, unmoving, patient and unceasing. The leopard had time, and he knew it.

Josh did not.

He looked over Ben's shoulder and smiled apologetically, agony written on the lines across his face. "Good luck," he whispered, as his hands began to slip.

"No!" Ben shouted, diving over the ledge. It was all I could do to hold his feet down, to keep him here with me, to save him when I couldn't save Josh.

No one could save Josh.

Emma's face crumpled as she heard the single scream when Josh hit the ground. Ben hung limply over the ledge, staring, and we both watched as the leopards dug their mouths into the soft skin of Josh's belly.

We watched the light bleed from his eyes.

We watched him die.

It took so much longer than I ever wanted to know for him to let go of his hold on life. He twitched spasmodically, fingertips tapping against the ground, and stared up at us, silent except for the sound of his breathing. I watched the blood gurgle from between his lips, foamy and thick. He was resigned to his fate, knowing that fighting would only prolong things—and all he could think of was us. He whispered "Go!" as loudly as he could, until he could speak no more.

Ben and I sat back against the ledge, staring into space, staring at Emma, who sat crying on the vent

I'd occupied only moments before. "I can't . . ." I whispered.

"I know," Ben said, and pulled me onto his chest. "He knew."

"I knew something was going to happen! I knew it!" I cried, pounding my fist on the roof. "I knew I should have gone last. It should've been me!"

"No," Ben said firmly, tears beginning to well in his eyes. "We talked about this. We wanted both of you to make it to safety, no matter what it cost. He knew he could do that much, and so do I. Don't let his sacrifice be in vain by saying it should have been you."

"Why the hell did you talk about this? Why do guys do that? Women and children are not that fucking important!"

Ben swallowed hard and closed his eyes. "Actually, considering this is a worldwide epidemic, I think "survival of the species" trumps "which one of us gets to live." That's why you're both important, Lens—because even if both of us die, you can go on."

"You're not dying!" I hit the roof again, sobbing, and held my arm out for Emma. "You're not dying."

"No," he murmured, as Emma crawled onto his lap next to me. I wrapped an arm around her, holding her closely as she shook. "No, I'm not dying. We're going to get out of here. We're going to honor what Josh did for us." Ben shook his head, determination shining in his eyes. "We're going to get out of here," he said again.

I took a shuddering breath and grabbed the vet wrap that I'd stuffed in my pocket. Vet wrap that Josh had gotten for me; vet wrap that he'd saved my life with. I began to wrap up my leg again, tightly, as I sat against Ben's shoulder and Emma's back. "I'm getting that stupid key," I said firmly. "I'm getting the key, we're finding Marley, and we're getting out of here."

Ben nodded, closing his eyes again. "But for now, I think we all need a minute," he admitted.

I said nothing as the three of us held each other, knowing that sooner or later, we'd have to get off the roof. We'd have to continue on and leave Josh here as food for the zombie leopards. We'd have to leave him behind and save ourselves without him, as he'd saved us. As I watched Emma cling to Ben, I resolved that come hell or high water, that little girl would be reunited with her Explorer troop, since I couldn't reunite her with her mother.

It was only a matter of time.

Day Four

The Last Stand (Part Three)

I could see the office buildings from where we stood, surveying the land. We'd taken the rope with us, wet with Josh's and my blood, and we began making plans for how, exactly, we were going to get the key to the loading dock. There was no way an animal could get through there on their own; concrete and wire might not stop them, but steel certainly could. If we only reached the loading dock, we'd be safe. Marley would be there, the rest of the kids and parents would be there, and someone with more experience being an adult than Ben and I had would know exactly what to do, and we'd be safe.

We started the slow trek on top of the tunnels, passing the empty wolf pen and moving on toward the coyotes. Most of our little coyote pack preferred beef to chicken, and I prayed at least some of the predator animals weren't zombies. Maybe we could theoretically save some of the animals, I reasoned.

We stopped on top of the coyote's section of the tunnel to rest my leg. I was beginning to believe that the worst was behind us—literally. We'd faced the lions, tigers, jaguars and leopards. We'd dealt with a zombie bear and zombie children. We knew where not to go and where we had to be in order to find safety, and we had a plan to get there. I was starting to galvanize myself, to put the tragedies of the last three days into a little box to hide them for good.

The night was beginning to become cold; Emma shivered in the moonlight, wrapping her arms around herself until Ben came forward and gave her his cardigan. "We're almost there," he promised. "We can do this."

We forgot about the owls.

The owls received mice, sure; they loved to chase the mice around their enclosures. It was enriching for them to chase and hunt live animals, but the large species of owls we housed needed more than the occasional mouse or two—so they got chicken, of course.

The owls were the second-to-last exhibit before we got to the office area. I peered carefully over the top of the roof, hoping that the exhibit was intact; it was reinforced netting, but we'd already discovered to what lengths animals would go to free themselves and the virus within them.

The owls were no exception to the rule.

The owls had formed a collective with the crows from the other side of the zoo, and they were currently perched on top of the tented netting, staring at us as we walked slowly across the roof, as far away from them as we could possibly be without falling off. "Please, God and Bob Ross, don't let them come near us," I whispered.

"Can we discuss this Bob Ross thing later? Because it's weird," Ben hissed. "We need to shut up and keep moving."

I was beginning to see that Emma was up way past her bedtime. She wavered on her feet, stumbling across the roof as we held her hands, and almost fell several times. It was about the same time that we decided she should ride on Ben's back that the crows and owls decided that we were fresh meat.

I could feel my stitches strain as we began to run, Ben carrying Emma. We were making pretty good time across the coyote tunnels until I realized that we were about to hit the giraffe section.

The one that required a ladder to get up onto the raised roof.

Because giraffes, obviously.

"I hate everything," I moaned, and grabbed the fanny pack from around Ben's waist. I began swinging wildly into the air, trying to create a safe haven of three feet or so for Ben to begin climbing.

Of course, he stood there staring at me like I'd lost my damn mind, until the first time the owl dove toward Emma with outstretched talons. "Shit," he said distractedly, staring up at the ladder.

"Get up the damn ladder!" I swung hard and hit a crow straight in its little beaky head, feeling vaguely satisfied as it fell to the ground.

Ben began to climb.

I had never been so thankful for the Explorer's club as I was then. First Aid was essential, yes; but they also learned something far more important—self-defense.

I was fairly certain that the pocket knife she brandished was NOT Explorer-approved gear, but I wasn't going to complain. I pulled my plastic rain jacket over my head as she swung her knife at the birds. The virus slowed their reaction time; they heaved their wings with labored squawks and hoots, screeching as the knife caught their wings.

I huddled beneath my jacket and began to climb, trusting a ten-year-old with what I hoped wasn't a plastic knife to defend me. I heard a yelp and feathers rained down, sticking to the yellow jacket. Emma and Ben reached the top of the short ladder with me right behind them.

Evidently, raptors and other predatory birds preferred to hunt out in the open. An owl with a ripped wing flew circles around Ben, who dropped Emma to the ground and shoved her toward me. I grabbed the rope we'd dragged with us and slung it around the light pole next to the roof.

"I'm gonna climb down and break the window, okay? When I call for you, climb down. It's only a few feet. Be careful of your arm, though."

I spread my jacket over Emma and she huddled in the corner of the roof, trying to look like a big yellow rock. As I looked up to check on Ben before Rope Climbing: Part Two, I could feel the color drain from my face. The only word for what the birds were doing was "swarming." It was almost incredible to see them knocking into each other, swooping down at Ben, turning to pick at each other's feathers mid-air, falling to the ground. "Ben! I screamed, and started to run toward him.

"Go! Get the damn window open!" he croaked ,fending off the birds with Emma's knife. I realized then that Dr. Warner had had our only gun. My heart sank. Blood ran down Ben's face in rivulets, and one eye squinted shut. My blood stilled and the world went quiet for me for one long moment.

Was it just saliva, or did talons carry the infection, too? More importantly, did birds salivate enough for it to saturate their beaks to transmit the infection?

Was Ben infected?

Birds littered the ground around his feet as he fought with an owl. I could almost feel its anger as it clawed at Ben's face, pecked at his skin. I couldn't tell if the pecks drew blood. Slowly I turned away from him, my heart aching, wishing I'd kept the fire axe from Mary's office. I stumbled over to the rope as quickly as I could.

I held onto the knot with both hands and swung hard with my good leg, knocking into the window as hard as I could.

Of course, it didn't break.

The anger I'd bottled inside the moment we figured out that we were truly fucked by zombies went up in flames. It wasn't fair that our zoo was one of the various "ground zeros" for a mistake we hadn't even made. Every person I knew who worked with us loved "their" animals to a fault. This wasn't our accident—but we'd still lost good people and almost all of our animals from the government's—or Corporate America's—stupid decisions.

Dr. Warner. Jeff. The parents, their children. Poor Mary, the office lady. Hank!

It was Hank that gave me the strength to move. I'd left him in the air vents with Marley, but I wasn't sure if cats could play follow the leader. He'd been my thesis buddy for so long now. My heart ached at the thought of him falling prey to these monsters.

I kicked at the window again and it finally shattered beneath my nearly-destroyed shoe. I used the heel to clear out the shards and gingerly sat on the sill. "Ben! Emma! Come on!"

Nothing happened.

"Ben!" I screamed into the darkness of the night. I listened closely and could only hear the beat of wings above me. I strained to hear any signs of someone human—Ben yelling, Emma's small voice, anything.

I froze. Did I need to go back up? More importantly, was I enough of a hero to risk getting out of here for Emma? For Ben?

The indecision was an immediate heavy weight upon me. I took a breath and held it, watching my hands shake on the windowsill. The real question was painfully honest: What kind of person did I want to be, now at the end of the world? I could run, lock myself in John's office and wait for help. I could forget any of this happened. I could let it go, and be safe.

I grabbed the rope.

#

"Lens! Move!"

Oh thank God. I heard Ben's voice as I was trying to figure out how to climb upward on a bum leg. I grabbed the first thing I saw—one of John's signed, large-print Stephen King books—and spread it over the windowsill to cover any glass I'd missed.

Ben twisted on the rope, struggling to hold on and hold Emma at the same time. He threw her into my arms and I held her tightly as she shivered.

When I looked up, I knew neither shivered from the cold.

Ben slid carefully into the room, landing heavily on John's desk, and sat, stunned, for at least a minute. I swallowed my exclamations, my fear, and stared up into his face.

Ben looked an awful lot like a zombie leopard I'd just recently spent some time with.

My hand flew to my mouth. I heard a low, heaving groan and startled, looking for the zombie—but it was me. I took a deep breath as I walked up to the desk. "How the hell do we fix this? What do we do?"

Ben sat quietly, in shock, hands held limply at his sides. I touched his shoulder gently as I inspected his face, his eye—the one that I'd thought had been closed against blood dripping into his eyes. I stared at him, looking at what the owl had done to it.

It wasn't gushing the way I would have imagined it. The socket of his eye still had a somewhat orb-shaped piece of dark pink and red tissue deep within a bloody hole. Strings of muscle and a clump of nerve dangled wetly, like the insides of a jack-o-lantern. Clear, viscous liquid had poured like candle wax down his cheek and dried there, leaving a sticky trail.

The owl had taken out his eye in its entirety.

"I don't know," he said woodenly.

I unzipped his fanny pack—it didn't seem quite so funny now—and started unwrapping a roll of gauze, forming it into a thick square. "I don't . . . I don't think I should use hand sanitizer on this," I said tentatively.

"No," he said, and cleared his throat. "Are you okay, Emma?"

She nodded, then blushed as she realized that he could no longer see her from where she was sitting. "Yeah, Mr. Ben," she said. "You saved me. Thank you for saving me." She paused, coming forward slowly, making sure to stay on his left side. She watched me doctor him gravely, stayed silent as I wrapped the vet tape around his head, securing a makeshift eye-patch-slash-bandage against the bloody hole. "You look like a pirate now," she offered tentatively.

His mouth twitched toward a smile and he winced as the movement pulled on the muscles near his eye. "Thanks, Emma," he replied, holding an arm out for her.

She rushed to him, and I saw her hiding the tears streaming down her face by burying herself in his side. "Are you okay? Really okay?"

Ben took a moment to consider, and I knew that he was going to give her the truth, whether it was good news or bad. "I think I will be," he said. "I don't know a lot about birds or viruses, but I think I don't need to worry about being infected by their feet."

"Talons," she corrected him primly.

"Talons," he agreed. "They pecked at me some, but I'm pretty sure their mouths were closed. I don't think I'm infected. I don't feel like I am."

"It really didn't take long for the infection to start hitting Jeff," I added quietly. "We'll know within an hour, probably."

I couldn't think about it for more than a minute at a time without my brain screaming at me. The thought of losing Ben was unbearable. He'd rescued me so many times without thinking of his own safety—I knew, then, how much he cared for me. I knew how important I was to him—and how special

Emma was becoming. My heart broke for the boy sitting silently on our boss' desk, blood seeping into the gauze as he comforted a worried little girl.

"Okay," I said, and took a deep breath. John had a rather impressive letter opener on his desk; clearly he had delusions of stealing The One Ring from Frodo and the hobbits and sojourning off to the mountain by himself. That is to say, I wielded a tiny sword that glittered in the fluorescent lights of the office as I knelt down, examining the drawers on his desk.

Most were unlocked and I rifled through them quickly. Paperwork, bills, an entire drawer full of Bill Nye, the Science Guy DVDs. I was learning things about John I never wanted to know. As I moved to the next drawer, I saw that this one was locked. "Bingo."

"Was his name-o," Emma whispered into Ben's side.

I guess songs carried over into zombie apocalypses just fine. I started to jiggle the knife in the lock, pushing it into the cracks of the drawer, anything I'd ever seen on TV for people to open things that they shouldn't open. Evidently the people on CSI had lied to me. I sat back on my heels, sighing heavily.

"Lens."

"What? Are you okay? Do you have aspirin? Oh my God, I can't believe I didn't ask you if you had aspirin. You need to take something. You need—"

Ben stood up slowly, wavering a little on his feet, and took the sword-thing from me. He knelt carefully by John's desk and inserted it in the cracks of the drawer. With a disconcertingly easy 'pop,' the drawer unlocked and slipped open.

"Well damn," I said after a long moment. "You've got skills."

He cleared his throat roughly. "I was an Explorer too," he said to Emma. "But you don't get this merit badge until you're a lot older."

I rummaged through the drawer. Employee files, key cards—a bill for hair loss medication?—and keys. Lots and lots of keys.

"Come on, really?"

"What?"

"He's got an entire fu—freaking pile of keys in here. Like, janitor-style huge key-rings full of keys of every kind." I glanced at Emma. It occurred to me how ridiculous it was to not swear around her when she was watching people die and get injured right and left, but it still felt wrong.

As I sat and stared at the pile of keys, it occurred to me that I wasn't sure who was responsible for Emma now that her mom was gone. From what

David had been saying, the world was pretty screwed. Almost everyone was coming down with zombie-itis. Ben and I might have been the only people Emma had left.

I looked at her, watching how carefully she hugged Ben, and realized that I was invested in this child now. I knew that the likelihood of her having family was getting slimmer with every moment that passed; even vegetarians and vegans that had never eaten chicken in their lives were at risk for getting attacked and turned, why not Emma's . . . whatever family she had left?

I met Ben's gaze above her head and knew he was thinking similar thoughts. Someone had to take care of this child, and at the very least, for now it was us. We would get her through this. She was so tough and so brave, even with her minor panic attacks. She had to survive; she had so much to offer this brave new world.

Or rotting, dead world. Your choice.

"What would a gate key look like?"

"Like it's way too old for the rest of the keys. It's a wrought-iron gate, remember?"

I nodded, filtering through the little pieces of metal that used to promise safety, security, and peace of mind. You could lock out everything that frightened you; stay away from the mass hysteria of society, if you chose to. Now we had zombie crows breaking through windows and people breaking down doors. Nothing was safe; nothing was sacred.

Not even us. I grabbed a few keys that looked like they'd match a wrought-iron gate and stood up slowly. "What's next?" I realized I'd never been to the loading dock before; not-zebras didn't get shipped to zoos, after all.

"We just have to get over the row of offices. The gate's on the other side." He paused and shifted Emma against him. She lay quietly across his bloody lap, eyes closed, fingers in her mouth. I wondered briefly if I would ever be capable of being that peaceful again.

I mentally toured the zoo, counting carnivorous animals as I went. Jaguars, tigers, lions, bears, birds . . . "So we're home free? Did you get all the crows?"

A small shudder ran down the length of his body. "Most of them," he said softly. "The rest of them started fighting over each other. I think we've run out of predators, for the most part."

I sighed in relief. There would be no more attacks; no more blood. Emma would be safe; we'd meet Marley at the loading dock and everyone would be safe there. We could just wait until someone came to rescue us. Everything would be fine now.

All we had to do was take a walk. I noticed, though, that Ben had taken John's prized slugger from off the wall and carried it over his shoulder. I suppose you couldn't be too careful.

Day Four

Dark of Night

We knew that Teddy was still in the tunnels; I could hear him over the air conditioning running into the office. His claws scraped against the concrete as he staggered around, sounding like steel meeting steel. Trying to navigate that particular hellhole with Ben's injury and mine sounded like a crisis waiting to happen, so back over the roofs we went.

I counted the buildings in my head as we traversed—John's office, cleaning supplies "closet," director of outreach, the collective office for all of the zookeepers. I could see the gates ahead of us; if I strained, I could almost hear voices, though that may have been wishful thinking.

The gates were on the other side of the aquatics supply office when we realized our mistake.

We'd never found the wolves.

Wolves absolutely did not deserve their bad rep; if I hadn't found my not-zebras, I would have adopted them as my own cause. They wanted nothing to do with humans; wolves in general were pretty peaceful animals, and their little nuclear family units (not so much a 'pack' unless using the loosest definition of the word) were adorable, with little fluffy puppies rolling around in their dens every spring. I knew wolves. I trusted wolves.

I did not trust zombie wolves.

Ben was right earlier; most of the predators we had were solitary hunters, with few exceptions. The foxes could have been a problem, but they'd taken care of themselves in their own gruesome little way, collapsing the den on top of themselves halfway through the quarantine. It was the wolves that hunted as a family unit, taking care that everyone received enough meat, that the hunt had been enough for all of their siblings, aunts and uncles.

The female head of the family stood in front of the pack, her fur bristling in thick spikes as she stared at the three of us. Father, siblings and children formed a tight "v" around her, spreading out so that we couldn't move forward if we'd tried.

Before I knew it, the wolves had circled around us, caging us in.

It broke my heart that they looked relatively well . . . and well-fed. They were infected, yes, but not yet dead. Their shining white eyes glittered in the moonlight as the female threw her head back and howled.

Even infected, it was the most beautiful sound I'd ever heard. Her pack, her family roared in triumph, howling to each other and the moon that they'd found what they were looking for. It was chilling to hear so many wolves at once; normally Ben and I were home at this time of night, and we missed the spectacle. I suddenly wished I could have missed it this time, too.

"How the hell did they get up here?" I sputtered. "Can wolves climb ladders now?"

"Probably one of the small herd animal habitats," Ben replied calmly. "They likely climbed up the fake mountain facade on the front and jumped onto the roof from there. There's a reason we don't have anything low enough for jumpers in the wolves' enclosure; they can jump a 10' fence if they want badly enough. That's why theirs are curved inward at the top with barbed wire."

"You seem pretty Zen for the fact that we're surrounded right now."

"You seem to want to hold a conversation in the middle of an emergency," he replied, and shoved Emma between us, putting him and I back to back around her.

"What the hell do you expect me to defend us with? I have a rope. Am I flinging rope at wolves now?"

Ben grimaced and pulled Emma's knife out of his pack, handing me the bat he'd been carrying. "Let's do this," he said decisively.

The wolves most definitely concurred.

The parents were crouched low to the ground as the teenage pups fanned around us. Huge canines were exposed as the wolves panted irregularly. I could almost see the mother, Storm, fighting the virus; she shook her head over and over again, backing up and moving forward the same two paces, refusing to signal her family to attack.

"Maybe we can walk through them," I suggested hesitantly. "She doesn't seem . . ."

The second I opened my mouth, Storm's son Xavier bolted forward quickly, pre-empting the attack. He buckled down in a low crouch, growling, so close that I could smell the sick scent of meat on his breath.

The bat made a sickening thud as it connected with his chest.

Xavier fell to the wayside and Storm took the opportunity upon herself to lead the attack. Two of Xavier's siblings fell upon him in his moment of weakness, burying their muzzles deep in the soft skin of his belly, and I could hear him yipping and whining as they tore him to pieces. Storm and Wolverine circled around to Ben's side.

Three wolves out of commission due to injury or zombie-ism. Four on Ben's side, three on mine, and Emma screeching between us. This was doable.

Storm's brother wasn't as coordinated as Xavier had been. He stumbled forward blindly, eyes unmoving and unseeing, snapping his teeth shut over and over again as he raged. He reared back and howled once more as he came toward me, snarling, and reached out to swipe at me with his massive paw. A nail reached out and tugged hard at my bandage, and I groaned, shuddering with the pain of the gauze being pulled off bloody skin.

I wound up and hit Cyclops as hard as I could. My bat connected with his head. I heard a yelp behind me as Ben dispatched one of the girls.

The remaining wolves circled again, regrouping, and I took a moment to breathe. It was a mistake; in that single moment, Rogue rushed me on unsteady feet from my side, knocking me onto the ground and crouching low on top of me. I held the bat in both hands, using it to push at her throat as I struggled, feeling the stitches in my thigh begin to swell and burst as I tried to get her off of me.

"Ben!" Emma yelled. "Ben! Lens is down!"

I saw Ben stab toward the other girl that had followed him and she backed off, circling again, as he hefted the knife in his hand. He tripped over the wolf in his quest to get to me, landing hard on his knees beside Rogue, blood beginning to trickle freely from his eye socket. He gasped raggedly as he got up, took a deep breath, and body-slammed Rogue into the ground.

I limped back to Emma as quickly as I could, walking around her in circles, trying to keep my guard up as I watched Ben struggle with Rogue. She tore at his shirt, ripping the zoo logo clear off of him, shaking her head viciously. She jumped onto his chest with an unsteady pounce like a fox, pinning him to the ground. A low growl sounded from her throat as she opened her mouth, her hot, stinking breath wafting onto Ben's face.

My bat grew slick with sweat and blood as I sought to protect Emma. I shoved her underneath me and crouched over her with the bat, swinging wildly as the wolves took turns rushing me, darting forward and back with far more coordination than the virus should have allowed. The scientist in me wanted to study why they were so much more efficient; the rest of me wanted to scream as two mouthfuls of jaws opened slowly and giant eyes stared up at me with what seemed like pure malice.

Tears streamed down my cheeks as I prepared for the end. I couldn't fend off all of these wolves by myself, and I couldn't leave Emma to save Ben; there was no way out. There was no way to salvage the situation. All I could do was hope that Emma fell under my body when it was over, hidden and safe beneath the death the wolves had wrought, until they gave up and left.

I heard the loud ratchet of a rifle and had to stifle a sob as I heard Marley's voice. "Not a chance, motherfuckers!"

Marley had come to save the day.

I would probably never find out why the loading dock crew had a rifle; if an animal prepped for transport to the exotic animal hospital was needed, perhaps, and the animal woke up. Maybe to deter workers from finding their slothfulness. Maybe someone just really liked guns. Either way, the loud booming thunder of a rifle shook the roof of the loading dock as Marley cycled the bolt in the rifle and shot again. My heart ached to see the wolves drop one by one—but not by much, considering one fell flat on Ben's face.

He screamed as a large wolf head came into contact with his beautiful, broken eye.

One of the parents poked their heads up the ladder and hesitated, seeing the carnage before us. "Is . . . is everything okay?"

I did sob this time, big heaving sobs as the last wolf fell and Emma rushed into my arms. Marley went to Ben and helped him heave the large male wolf off of his face. She said nothing upon seeing his makeshift eye patch; simply raised a brow, made an "arrr" pirate noise, and helped him to his feet.

We helped each other down the ladder and into the loading dock. I saw the burst air vent that they must have climbed out of; it was an impressive distance from the floor, and I was pretty proud as I surveyed the crowd of our survivors. Marley hadn't lost a single one.

I closed my eyes briefly, wishing we could say the same. Dr. Warner's death would haunt me for the rest of my life. I would see the sacrifice he'd made for me every night as I went to sleep. I wondered if he knew that he was going to die when he'd decided to help us cross the way we did, or if he was as surprised as the rest of us.

"Where'd you get the gun?" Ben asked.

"Believe it or not, the loading dock crew had a whole bunch of useful stuff down here," Marley explained. "There's more fire axes, saws, tools, all sorts of things."

"How long have you been here?"

She frowned, looking out the high windows at the lack of light. "It took about three hours to get everyone through the vents. We had a couple more fall-throughs, but they were in places where we could shore up furniture and get back up." She paused, biting her lip. "I'm pretty sure the adults are okay, but we saw some stuff that no one should have to see. The carnivores went wild."

"We lost Dr. Warner," I told her, looking over at Emma. She'd rushed over to the group of Explorers, assuredly explaining her adventures to all of her friends. She kept looking back at Ben and I, however; I had a feeling that we would be seeing a lot of Emma in the very near future.

"How?"

I told her the story without embellishment. I recapped everything that had happened since we'd split up; the tigers, the leopards, the crows—the veritable zoo (no pun intended) of animals that had made it their personal mission to eat us. I watched Ben out of the corner of my eye; he sat silently on the edge of the loading dock, staring at the truck doors, frowning.

He stood up carefully and turned to the crowd, waiting until they noticed him. There were about 26 of us left now, children and adults; it wasn't a huge crowd, but it felt like it in the small space we were in. "We've got the keys. I'm going to open one of the truck doors, and Marley and I are going to check out the outside. We'll signal for you if everything's clear, okay?"

I gave Ben his baseball bat back and offered him the keys I'd stolen. "Be careful, okay? You really shouldn't continue playing the hero after everything that's happened. You need to rest."

"I'll rest once we figure out what the hell is going on outside," he said grimly. "Have you gotten any more emails from David?"

I gasped, searching my pockets frantically for my phone. "Shit. No, I think I lost my phone somewhere around the first time my stitches popped open. Speaking of which, do you have any vet tape left?"

Ben winced and sighed. "Well, it would have been too good to be true to have contact with the outside," he replied.

I grabbed his hand and he helped me up onto the loading dock. I waved my hands widely, trying to get the attention of the adults, and waited until they quieted again. "Does anyone have cell phone service right now?"

Two adults and one little boy raised their hands.

"Great. Go ahead and check the news for us while Ben and Marley open the door, all right?" They nodded, and I hopped down to meet with them. Any possible warnings about what was going on outside those gates would be a blessing unparalleled.

What really worried me was that we were far enough outside of city limits that we were in farm country. I didn't anticipate many cows, steers, or horses were fed chicken, but what if they were infected by their owners? What if we had a zombie herd of cows waiting for us outside the gate?

"CNN says that the airports are all closed down . . ."

"Fox News says that everything's fine, they're starting to get quarantines up . . ."

"MSNBC says that the government hasn't given an update in hours, that we're on our own . . ."

"Hey, does anyone with Northern Link have reception? Mine just went down . . ."

As much as I despised the normal news channels, I had to give credit to the last one; it sounded the most feasible. I didn't doubt that the White House was probably torn to shreds by this point; the Secret Service could only take care of so many threats at once before they, too, were overwhelmed.

What overwhelmed me were the number of people reporting that entire phone networks were seemingly down. If even cell phones weren't working . . . How quickly had this spread?

Ben and Marley nodded to each other firmly. Ben had eschewed the baseball bat for one of Marley's fire axes; I couldn't blame him. They hefted their weapons and rolled open the door.

#

Emma had come back to sit next to me once Ben and Marley were gone. The loading area wasn't large, but it did have an awful lot of bushes for potential danger to hide beneath. I wasn't sure how to answer her when she asked how long Ben would be gone.

"Emma? What other family do you have? Do you have brothers or sisters? A daddy? Another mom?"

She shook her head slowly, putting her fingers into her mouth again. "I had a daddy once but he left when I was really little. My mom said we didn't need one because we were best friends and could take care of ourselves." She paused. She looked so small sitting on the large wooden crates that decorated the loading dock; I knew she was ten, but somehow I wanted to comfort her, to make everything better for her, and I knew that I couldn't.

"Do you have cousins? Aunts or uncles?"

"I have uncle Bryan and uncle Joseph but they live really far away," she said. "They took me to Disney World once. It was really neat. They had these pirates, do you think Ben could be a pirate there? I bet he's so sad that he hurt his eye and needed an eye patch, but I bet we could get him a job at Disney World and . . ."

It was amazing how much one little girl could talk when the bulk of her fears were released. We were relatively safe in the loading dock; she could see the heavy locks on the doors, and she knew Ben and Marley were right outside. Suddenly, she was safe and sound, and neither one of us knew what to do with ourselves except stare awkwardly at the concrete floor.

"I think he'd like it if you helped him get used to it," I finally replied. "He's going to have some trouble figuring out how far away things are for awhile, and we need to make sure to keep it clean so he doesn't have an infection. We're going to have to go to a drug store and . . ."

I stopped mid-sentence, frowning. Was that even a thing? Did drug stores still exist? We'd been locked in the zoo for four days, according to my watch. It had finally gone from "technically morning but still dark" to "the sun's starting to come up," and I felt relieved. I wasn't sure if the virus would allow these animals to return to their nocturnal state and leave us the hell alone, but I hoped with all I had that this was the end.

Not that end. The good type of end.

I watched the Explorers and their parents mill about the dock, opening boxes and drawers and generally being normal children and adults in the wake of such a disaster. I wandered over to the door that Ben and Marley had opened and leaned hard against the wall, blinking tears out of my eyes.

Even this far away from the city, I could see the smoke. I could see the burning buildings before us; I could identify the tiny places where I'd spent so much time. Up the hill and to the left was where my apartment lied, housing pretty much video games and thesis papers. I felt a lump in my throat as I realized, finally, that my dream had died the moment Patient Zero had. If the world had plummeted into such disaster in a measly four days, the likelihood of airports ever running again was slim to none. I would never find Africa. I would never find my Quaggas. Everything I had been working for, for the last eight years, was gone.

I sat down abruptly, burying my face in my hands. It seemed so insignificant in the face of the tragedy; what were a couple not-zebras in Africa compared to the entirety of American culture failing? I knew my priorities were skewed. But it still hurt, and I had to acknowledge that. Even in the middle of a pandemic, I could suffer and grieve for the dreams I had that had died with the virus, never to be resurrected.

I lifted my head once more and spotted my college, burst into flames. A sob escaped my lips as I sat quietly next to the door, waiting for Marley and Ben to come back. Somehow, it was the college's destruction that cemented the disaster for me. Nothing would ever be the same again. Nothing was the same now.

I watched as Ben and Marley came trudging back, eyes averted. They didn't look any bloodier or dirtier than they had going; I took that as a good sign.

It was not a good sign. Because of course it wasn't.

"What." I said flatly.

Ben looked as if he were struggling to raise a brow, but realized how bad of an idea optional facial expressions were at this point in his life. "Is it that obvious?"

"Pretty fucking obvious. What's wrong?"

Ben and Marley sat down next to me, politely ignoring the tears I was viciously wiping with the least bloody corner of my shirt. I began unwrapping my thigh to doctor up what the ladders, the running, and the wolves had undone—but mostly to give me something that would let me not look at the faces of my best friends when they gave me news I didn't want to hear.

"Well . . . you know the highway? The one you can see from the back gate?"

"Not really. I never come in that way. I like—liked to say hi to Mary on my way in. But assuming I know what a highway is and where it's located, yes, go on."

Marley heaved a breath. "There are cars all over the place. It looks like a parking lot in the middle of an earthquake. Cars are stopped everywhere, spun around, it looks like everybody lost their damn minds."

"And?"

"What, that's not enough?"

"A parking lot full of cars wouldn't make you come back so soon."

Marley paused as Ben moved over to sit next to me, putting an arm around my shoulder. "Good point," she said. "The problem is *why* people stopped in the middle of a highway."

"Marley, can you just tell me? Because I don't have the patience for this suspense shit."

Ben interrupted. "The only thing we could figure out is that some of the people from the farms ended up heading toward the city, attracted by the fires. If you squint really hard, you can see crowds of people hovering by burning buildings. But that's not the problem. The problem is what happened when the farmers and their families got to the city."

"Oh, shit, there's a park right there."

"There's a park right there," he confirmed. "You can see the fence from here. We're not *that* far out of the city. I think what happened is that the infected from the farms went into the city, infected the people in the park and anyone trying to get out, and as people tried to run and get out of their cars . . ."

"They got infected, too. Wait, you're telling me that everyone and everything we know is now on the other side of a football field that used to be a highway, and it's full of zombies?"

Marley sighed, rubbing her temples with her fingertips. "I thought we could open the gates and sneak around to the front of the zoo and leave from there—but there are a few problems. Where would we go? The nearest town is miles away. We'd have to walk that whole way with a bunch of kids and freaked out parents."

"What's the other problem?"

The look on Ben's face was similar to the one he always gave me when he didn't want me to know what was going on. It was a cross between swallowing a lemon and feeling constipated. "The people from the highway are coming this way. There are safety spotlights as part of the security system that run all night long, and I assume they were attracted to the light. If we're going, we have to go now."

"And you fucking take twenty minutes to tell me this when we need to get the hell out of here?" I struggled to finish wrapping my thigh in a hurry, until Ben took the tape away from me. He tilted his head so that his good eye could focus on the wrap, and began to doctor my leg.

"We've got enough time to fix your leg, at least," he murmured. "I'm going to wrap it tight enough to give it more support than you had before. I think Emma's painkillers are starting to wear off; she looks like she's going to cry. I'm going to go give her some aspirin; can you make the announcement?"

I tried to smile through the fear, thinking about how gently Ben was treating Emma. It scared me in more ways than one that I thought he'd be a great father. I slowly stood up on top of the platform and put my dirty, disgusting fingers in my mouth, whistling shrilly.

"HEY! We've got a problem. We found the back gate, we have the key, but we've got a bunch of zombies headed this way. Our options are to stay here and hope the gate holds, or to get out quick and head around to the front of the zoo and hope nobody's coming toward us that way, and that none of the animals know how to use a turnstile. Stand over here on the left for stay, stand over here on the right to go."

I watched each parent looking at their child—and the parents that had no child to look after. Their faces crumpled with the reminder, and I wasn't sure how I could ever fix this situation. None of this should be my responsibility—but it was. Everyone begs the universe that they wouldn't be the one asked to rise up. All of us wish that we could stay low and out of sight, not responsible for others, waiting for someone else to take the lead and show us what to do.

Sometimes there was no one to wait for, because the person that was meant to take charge was you.

I counted quickly, glancing at the parents that looked back and forth between each other. I could tell that they didn't want to be in charge of this decision; many people shuffled toward the middle in indecision, tossing the life preserver out to me to catch so that they wouldn't have to drag me to the boat.

"All right," I sighed, and went to the small arsenal of strange weapons that Marley had acquired throughout her examination of the loading dock. "Every parent, grab a weapon. We've got bats, pipes, axes, two guns—do what you can. Use what you can. We're going out the gate and we're going to try to head to the next town over. Maybe they fared better than we did."

After all, they couldn't fare much worse. Could they?

Day Four

The Daring Escape

My scientist's brain began cataloging the different types of zombies that we'd run into. The first was the type who'd had the virus and the chicken—still living, for the most part, but definitely not "alive and well," so to speak. The second were what worried me; those were the "living dead" type zombies, the ones who had gotten bitten or attacked and had died, only to rise again.

It must have been the second type that had begun to follow us through the back of the zoo and into the forest to the west. Every movie, TV show and zombie book I'd ever experienced taught me that zombies were afraid of water—but not our zombies. I watched as the horde behind us approached the small river, walked straight into it up to their shoulders, and disappeared straight down into the mud. They presumably marched right across the bottom of the river, appearing no worse for the wear on the other side.

I was thankful that there wasn't an overabundance of athleticism in our little plague-ridden piece of humanity. The zombies were persistent, true, but they weren't particularly fast. We were making good time toward the front of the zoo; Marley had even begun to smile, a rare occurrence even when everything was all right. It was, of course, when we began to let our guard down that we reached the corner that we would round to get to the front gate.

I carefully walked toward Marley, seeing the look on her face and not wanting to alarm any of the parents. In what would be a truly jackassed move, I realized that Ben couldn't see me when I was on the right side of his body; he hadn't noticed that I'd moved away until I was already gone. I pulled Marley aside and frowned. "What's the look on your face? What's happening right now that I don't want to know about?"

Marley carefully guided me by the shoulders until I could barely see around the corner. The front gates of the zoo were nearly overrun; I counted six policemen. I saw the rest of the parents that had been called when we'd hidden in the aquarium, ready to come retrieve their sick children from what had only seemed like an inconvenience at the time. Word had gotten out; I saw a Channel Six news van sitting askew in the parking lot, nearly knocked on its side by the crew that were currently trying to end the screams of the woman inside.

She lay on what was now the floor of the van, convulsing and twitching uncontrollably, shrieking at the top of her lungs. Moment by moment, I could see the situation shifting. As they fought her, fought to keep her quiet, she almost seemed to grow in strength; she overpowered one, then another, and then she wasn't the only one screaming anymore.

Marley bit her lip, aimed, and shot. She shot once, missed; two more times; three. The rest of the crew fell to the side of the van, sobbing.

It seemed like a good idea at the time. Ending the woman's suffering was a noble thing to do. It was not, however, the most intelligent of decisions. As Marley began to lower the rifle, the zombies began to turn.

They spotted us.

We came together, forming a ring around most of the children—except the ones that refused. Four of the kids—including Emma—had spirited away some of the weapons that we'd found in the loading dock, and were in fine fighting form. There was no fear in the eyes of the four ten-to-twelve year old children that stood amidst us; I hesitated, then, to even call them children. They were the Advent of the Apocalypse; part of our murderous menagerie. These newly fledged barely-young-adults would be the ones who rose out of the ashes of what we had wrought. If anything would come after what our hubris had caused, it would be them that created it.

It seemed unfair to say anything, to do anything else but to let them fight with us.

Emma brandished a small hatchet—and I wondered how in the hell she'd hidden that from us on the walk around the building. Brandon, who had seen his parents and Mrs. LeDoux attempt to eat flamingos, held a rubber mallet. Kelsey, whose twin sister had attacked her on the way to the tunnels, wielded a MagLite bigger than she was. And for reasons I couldn't explain, a fierce little girl dressed all in black had a fire extinguisher.

All right, then.

Our zombies weren't at the stage yet where they were rotten, maggot-filled representations of humanity; thankfully, I wasn't sure if they ever would be. I had a small, secret hope that if we were to truly see the zombie apocalypse the way it was always represented, that I would not be around to see it. It was the first time I admitted to myself that I might not want to see the future that these kids created out of the present that we'd fucked up.

Regardless of their lack of maggot-itude, the shamblers that were coming toward us were not the most welcoming sight I'd ever seen. One parent still held her Coach purse over her shoulder; it was only absurd due to the thick, bloody lines carved into her chest by infection-desperate claws. I saw the deep punctures of canine wounds embedded in her shoulder and knew they would reach around to the other side. It was a miracle the purse wasn't shorn as well.

I blinked, shaking my head. I knew cognitively that it was a coping mechanism to focus on the absurd, but the realities of a zombie with a toupee was too surreal even for me. I hefted my trusty baseball bat that I'd retrieved before we'd left the docks and took a deep, grounding breath.

When the rest of us stood still, quavering under the gaze of more than a baker's dozen of the technically undead, it was, of course, the little ninja with the fire extinguisher that made the first move. With a determined shriek that sent tendrils of liquid thrill up my spine, she charged the man whose toupee was hanging askew from a skull battered and torn by talons and swung the extinguisher by its handle. The tank rocketed through the air and connected with a sturdy thunk.

The zombie stood still, rocking back on his loafers. A low, gurgling groan emitted from his lips, spittle flying freely from split lips. I didn't have a moment to worry about what that may have meant as the crowd began a slow, steady charge.

I couldn't worry about anyone other than myself, not even Emma and Ben. I moved to give myself enough room to swing and suddenly, it was time. A woman rushed forward, snarling through twisted lips, and reached toward me with one arm attached by mere muscle and sinew. I rolled my shoulders and tried to remember the one lesson my father had ever given me on softball.

I swung. I swung and connected with a meaty 'thwack,' watching briefly as she stumbled back, her arm coming loose and falling to the grass. The mom next to me hefted a pipe, twisting her hands to grip it, and buried the thick metal in the skull of a man she'd likely known for her child's entire school career.

Knowing this, knowing that these people could be husband and wife; that they'd served on the PTA together; made cookies together almost drove me to my knees. There were so many sacrifices for something people wrote hundreds of horrible young adult books about; the zombie apocalypse. As much as I'd joked, it still hurt to know that nothing would ever be the same.

My bat connected and a man's head finished severing from its neck; it rolled swiftly toward the forest, and three infected followed. I yelled to Marley, "How's it looking from that side?"

"About like we're boxed in by fucking zombies so I'm a little busy here, Lens!"

I couldn't help grinning. Adrenaline rushed through my body as I hit another zombie out of the park.

My smile died when we lost the first on our side.

One of the dads was losing a wrestling match between himself and someone he obviously knew well; tears slid down bloodied cheeks, dirt staining his face. He struggled with the woman, locking arms with her, almost hugging her in his quest to keep her snapping teeth away from his throat.

Fear hit me hard. I wondered then if the infected had strength that far surpassed ours, or if they simply didn't care when tendons tore and snapped. When I heard her ribs cracking and popping as she shoved past his hold and began to tear into his throat, I knew it didn't matter. We were outnumbered, and out-gunned.

Once the first man went down, it was as if the seal had been broken. I heard a strangled sob and saw the little boy go down hard, a veritable pile of zombies burying him for good. Another woman screamed as she slipped, burying her own fire axe in her chest. I turned and saw one of the children being torn; she was a husk, thank God, as she was rent limb from limb. The zombies strained as they fought over the body, and her arm came free with a slurp and a pop.

Only Emma and the ninja were left from the children that had volunteered to fight. We were dropping like flies. I looked up to find Ben next to me, his face grim as he held his rifle, head cocked to the side to compensate for his eye. I was so proud of him as I watched him out of the corner of my eye issuing instructions, firing carefully at zombies he was sure he could hit.

I heard Marley scream, and only had a brief moment to beg the universe that it wasn't her, that by the end of this, she would stand next to me with a sardonic smile and a 2x4 she stole from the loading dock. The circle tightened around the kids that needed protecting, and I saw Emma dispatch Mrs. LeDoux with a sad grimace. I was beyond proud of her; she was one of the strongest people I knew, fighting with a simple hatchet and a broken arm.

The sun had risen by the time it was over. The infected parents and kids had been dealt with, and one Explorer troop leader had led the children toward the forest while Marley and one of her sidekicks tried to put a bullet into the brains of the ones who had fallen on our side as quietly as possible.

Unfortunately, rifles were far from silent.

All told, out of around 32 parents and kids, we'd lost twelve adults and five children, including my little ninja friend. Emma had been the only fighting Explorer to survive. We sat in a loose circle at the edge of the woods, staring at the bloody dirt, unwilling to discuss or think about the carnage we had just unleashed.

I had asked myself what kind of person I wanted to be in this new world, potentially lawless and most certainly never to be the same. As we looked around sheepishly, the realization sunk in.

We were killers.

#

We had no real food, little water, and only half of us had working weapons. We had Ben's, Emma's, and a few scattered Explorer and Explorer Parent's fanny packs with granola bars, mini bottles of water, a few small pocket knives (which cemented the belief that Emma's was definitely not Explorer approved) and a few random tools like flashlights, gauze, duct tape, and other useful odds and ends.

Put together it sounded like a lot. Set out in front of us, we were screwed.

"All right," Marley said, holding up a bloody hand for attention. "We pretty much can't stay here, or we're eventually going to get eaten. The plan is the next town over—Woodbury—in hopes they've got working phones, or water, or some kind of fortification. Maybe a hospital; I know they've at least got a clinic. Agreed?"

Most of us nodded, with very little objection. I was beginning to find that if someone sounded vaguely authoritative in a crisis, most of the time, people would blindly follow. It was likely how we'd gotten into this situation in the first damned place: one person just following the leader, following instructions without question, not even realizing that one decision made by their superior in an office they'd never been to could cause them to murder most of the world.

I wondered if the person who had ultimately performed the act, who had injected the chicken or created the virus in a lab knew what their creation had wrought—or if, like our entire zoo, had become one of the lost.

I shook my head and realized that Marley had been talking all along. We all stood up slowly, some of us more agile than others, and began to make our way down the small road in front of the zoo.

Ben reached over and held my hand as I limped my way forward. I couldn't fathom how much pain he must be in; blood and viscous fluid leaked slowly down his cheek as I watched, wanting nothing more than to wipe the hurt away. As I winced, stepping on a rock and jarring my leg, he offered me a small smile, and I knew he felt the same.

We walked hand in hand towards the rising dawn of the fourth day of the new world, watching Emma point at and identify various plants for our viewing pleasure. I marveled at how little she seemed to feel her arm; she was just happy to be outside and able to use what she'd learned. I looked over at Ben, who had apparently forgotten and put me on the side he couldn't see from. I smoothed my bloody jeans down with my free hand as I contemplated our futures and frowned, finding a lump in the watch pocket.

I pulled my hand out and smiled.

Day Five? Six?

Blood and Bones

We had walked for miles; one of the little boys' watches evidently tracked such things, and it claimed we had gone eight miles by the time the sun reached its full height in the sky. The weather was thankfully cool; we were beaten and battered, bloody and broken, but the good news was that it wasn't 90 degrees out and we hadn't seen a zombie near or far for six miles.

We were far enough away that it seemed like a good time to stop and lick our wounds. I reached toward Ben's face, intent on cleaning his wound, but he shied away.

"Is this some kind of macho thing? Like you don't want me to take care of you? Or is it that you don't want to show weakness? Because if that's it, I'm gonna kick your alpha male ass so hard-"

He flushed, looking down with his good eye. "Neither," he said quietly. "I just think I bled enough that the gauze is probably . . . you know . . . stuck. And I'm kind of freaked at how bad that might hurt."

I immediately felt like the biggest asshole in the world. Of *course* he was afraid. He was probably already in an incredible amount of pain, with dried, bloody gauze stuck inside of a torn socket. I couldn't even think of what it felt like to either have the optic nerve exposed or completely yanked out. "I'm sorry," I said. "I just . . . really want to help somehow, and I don't know what to do. You've saved me so many times in this whole fucking mess. You saved Emma. I can't even think of how to express—"

I closed my eyes, holding his hand tightly. I'd never thought our problems would ever be worse than arguing over pizza about his Xbox problem or my living like a hobo. Now, we had faced life and death, together. What a way to cement a relationship, I thought.

"Don't," he said abruptly. "This is just the beginning, Lens. There's no telling what more might happen. Society's gonna fail; we've lost the government, we're already losing technology, and we're going to have to figure out how to live off the land or where to steal non-perishables if this shit goes much farther. There's no telling what's coming." He swallowed audibly, Adam's apple bobbing wildly. "And you might not want . . ."

"So help you God and Bob Ross-"

"Seriously with the Bob Ross right now?"

"-and Bob Ross, Benjamin Hebert, I will strangle you myself if it stops you from saying something as stupid as what was about to come out of your mouth."

He blushed again and managed half a smile from the non-damaged side of his face. "Thanks, Lens."

"Are you . . . okay, though? Marley told me the last time the Explorers came through that a few of the moms were, uh, packing some serious pills."

He looked up at me hopefully, his good eye glistening with tears. "Please?" It was all he said.

I immediately stood up and went over to Marley. "I need a favor," I murmured.

She was using one of the Explorer's duct tape to bandage a slash across her waist. "If I can, I will. What's up?"

"Ben is in some serious distress. Is there any way we can take up a collection of pills or something from the Explorer moms?"

She offered a fiendish grin. "Now why didn't I think of that?" she crowed. "There's got to be a stockpile out here enough to stone a horse."

"Excuse me!" she hollered immediately. "We're going to take an inventory and divvy up our items by type. I need medications in this pile, especially anything useful for the wounded! Anything that can be used for bandaging over here in this pile . . ."

It didn't take more than five minutes—after a few hushed conversations with some of the mothers who hadn't truthfully emptied their purses—for Marley to hightail it back over to me and Ben. "I've got Vicodin and some codeine," she offered proudly. She paused. "And something that I'm pretty sure is for a dog, but we could try it, I guess."

Ben swallowed the codeine dry and gave us both a thankful smile. "I've tried not to bitch about it, but this is pretty much the worst thing I've ever felt in my life," he said.

"I'm so sorry, Ben. If we'd only gotten the shot gun . . . if I hadn't listened to you and came to help . . ."

Ben sighed. "Then Emma might be dead, or you, because no one would have gotten the damn window open. Don't feel bad. You did exactly what needed to be done."

"Pragmatic, that's me," I muttered, but Ben was no longer listening. I assumed at that point he was chasing zombie butterflies that the rest of us couldn't see.

When we finally chose one person per item type (I got to have an entire fanny pack full of duct tape), we started on once more. We managed another 9 miles before our wounded—especially me, who'd taken the Vicodin for my leg—collapsed in a heap of exhaustion. We'd walked until we found a deserted gas station on the seldom-used road. Thankfully, it seemed as if the owners had booked it when news of the virus had hit—the door wasn't even locked.

We piled inside and shimmied the bars over the doors before sighing in relief. It was relatively safe there; there was plenty of . . . well, edibles, even if you might not be able to technically call it food. There were travel pillows and packs of diapers to be used as travel pillows as we all picked an aisle to set up shop for the night. As we all lay, tossing and turning on the floor, I turned to Ben.

"Ben?"

"Yeah, Lens?" His voice was tight. I knew the codeine must be wearing off.

"About Emma . . ."

He turned to face me. "She's got no one, doesn't she."

"No, she doesn't." I looked at the little girl who was currently using my butt as a pillow as I lay on my side. "I mean, the other kids either have a live parent or know somebody here, but her . . ."

"She seems to have latched onto us," he agreed.

I was silent for a long time, staring at a rack of beef jerky behind Ben. "It's something to think about," I said cautiously.

"It's something to think about," he echoed softly. "Good night, Lens."

I wondered if he knew that Emma had woken up, and heard our contemplations. As I lay quietly, she snuggled closer to me, skirting the thigh wound I'd gotten, and briefly hugged me around the waist.

Something to think about.

#

It took us another two days to creep along the thin, twisting road and come to Woodbury. It seemed as a number of various concerned citizens had left their cars in the middle of the road, fleeing from a place that, as it turns out, wasn't the only one with problems. Woodbury was . . .

Well. Woodbury was still there; at least it had that going for it.

There were home-made signs stuck up on the large metal one that welcomed us to Woodbury, population 3,601. I wondered if the "one" felt lonely, or if it was an honor to be singled out on what was effectively the world's blandest billboard. The little wavering pieces of paper stuck to it were lost and found signs—except everyone was only lost.

"Looking for my mother . . ." "Missing: 38 year old man . . ." The worst were the children, both those missing and the ones who had written their posters in crayon, looking for their own family members. Emma wasn't the only one who had lost her family—or as much of her family as we knew about—in this mess. I only hoped that Cornerhouse Zoo wasn't the beginning of this mess; ground zero had to be somewhere else, right?

As we passed by the sign and walked into the town proper, I heard the now-familiar clicking of rifles and shotguns. Evidently, Woodbury no longer welcomed visitors quite as nicely as they used to.

"Come on down to the pharmacy really slowly, ladies and gentlemen. Put your hands above your heads and follow the man in the blue shirt," an unknown voice called.

"This is ridiculous," I whispered to Ben, hooking my baseball bat through the handle of my now-defunct laptop bag. "What the hell are we gonna do, rob the place?"

He glanced over at me, hands raised lazily above his head. I knew that it was an act; he was saving the codeine for the moments he really needed it. We needed proper medical care, and fast. I couldn't believe that with all of the parents and adults we'd gathered—zookeepers that Marley had picked up along the way, Explorer troop parents—that we hadn't at least accidentally found our way to a nurse or an EMT. Apparently the Explorer parents were a pretty vanilla-flavored group.

"I'm beginning to believe that we aren't in our little zoo anymore, Toto," he said quietly. "I think they *are* worried about our little band of merry zoo-goers. They probably have supplies and stuff we didn't have at the zoo—supplies that they won't want to share, if it comes down to it."

I was baffled. Maybe it was growing up with an exotic vet—my childhood viewpoint was probably a little skewed. Maybe it was living in a dorm for seven years with a bunch of science nerds. Regardless of the reason, I couldn't imagine living in a place where there wasn't at least one person willing to—well, at least willing to not put a gun to your head on principle.

I guessed that was a wee bit much for Woodbury.

"That's right, nice and easy." We were herded toward a pharmacy with broken windows, boarded over. As I looked around, trying to seem as harmless to the men with guns as I possibly could, I saw what could only be described as roadblocks stretching from building to building, as if they were barricading the residents in.

Or keeping something else out.

The pharmacy was near the first roadblock to the west exit of the small town. It wasn't exactly the barricade I'd make, but at this point, I assumed beggars couldn't be choosers. The barricades were made of two cars each, crumpled but still usable as the base for their fortifications. Large pieces of plywood had been anchored to the roofs and hoods of the cars, shored up with 2x4s that still had tags from the local hardware store. Barbed wire completed the ensemble. I genuinely wondered if zombies had learned how to parkour or something, because I sure as hell couldn't imagine Mary or Mrs. LeDoux crawling up a bare piece of plywood.

Then again, I was disturbingly used to zombie tigers and bears at that point, so perhaps my vision of what could and could not launch itself over barbed wire was slightly skewed.

We clambered into the pharmacy, piling in between emptied shelves and those full of items that the town had apparently deemed useless; pregnancy tests, condoms, little pill containers. I made a note in the back of my head to knock down a pharmacy—hey, maybe this pharmacy!—if this truly was the end of civilized life. I was pretty sure somebody, somewhere would trade food for . . . well.

The gun to my head sort of answered the 'civilized

life' question. "What do you want? What are you doing here?"

It had been four—five?—days since the beginning of the end at the zoo, and over a week since the first of the epidemic had been announced on the news. How far had we really fallen in such short of a time?

The man with the gun wore blue jeans, the kind that were faded at the knees from working hard, and dirty. His calloused hands told me he knew the value of hard work; he held the rifle steadily, and he looked rather comfortable with the thought of blasting a hole through the back of my head.

Well, wasn't this just swell. Marley stepped forward ,taking a breath and putting on her 'I'm here to show screaming little girls baby snakes' voice. "We just escaped from Cornerstone Memorial Zoo. Which, by the way, it's probably a bad idea to visit it at this point. Have you seen anything in the woods? Zombie bears, for instance? Because we've been dealing with zombie fucking wolves, so we're just a little tired at this point. We've got one woman who needs new stitches and probably crutches, a little girl who would really like a better cast than a spatula and duct tape, and someone who has been quietly dealing with the pain of *getting his damn eye ripped out by a zombie owl* for the past, what, two, three days?"

She glanced at me for confirmation and I nodded, impressed with her composure. I'd heard a Marley tantrum before when something happened to one of her snakes, or at the stupidity of parents who encouraged fear of reptiles in their innocent children—this, however, was Marley in fine form, a Marley who was kicking ass—and there would be no names to take.

"So he's got a giant, gaping hole in his head. I've got at least four people who now need bandages and a tetanus shot. We've got at least one more broken bone, scratches and sprains, and I'm lucky my guts aren't spilling out of my abdomen. Is that *okay* with you? Are our injuries *enough* for you to be willing to deal with? Because we came here knowing that there was a fairly decent medical clinic here."

She gestured at Hank, who rubbed around her ankles. The stoic cat had made it through the tunnels and followed us the entire way to Woodbury, making the rounds past each injured and traumatized child in some weird pecking order that only he understood. "We also need a veterinarian, because they usually have good cat food, and Hank fucking deserves cat food. So put the gun down. My name's Marley."

Mr. Blue Jeans raised a slightly bushy eyebrow. "That's what you say when someone's got a gun to your head?"

Marley didn't so much as blink. "That's what I'd say whether you were naked and screaming or holding a knife to my throat, yes."

A thin smile lit his face. "I have a feeling we're going to have a love-hate relationship, Ms. Marley, and I'm not entirely sure which way it's going to lean."

I cleared my throat loudly and stepped forward. I had no words to soothe either one of them, no magic balm that could make them get along—but I did have my own card to play.

I gently pulled Ben forward to stand next to me and took a deep breath. Ben stood silently, though I could feel him shaking beside me. I knew there was something behind that pharmacy counter that would help him—so the card was played, the one not even he knew about.

As the man in blue jeans swiveled—his gun coming with him—I rolled up the inch or two of "shorts" I had on my left leg and carefully began to unwind the bandages. In rather short order, I exposed the leopard strike to the air and winced at the cool breeze.

The man stared at my leg for a long moment, his face blank, lines smoothed. Four stitches had come loose in the final battle against the infected, and I hadn't been able to bring myself to pull the sides together and duct tape it. A three-inch gaping tear was ringed by a crusted yellow at the edges. It seeped a viscous fluid, sticky and slightly foul-smelling, mixed with blood, old and new. Small lines of red radiated outward from the center, and I knew I must have fever-bright eyes.

"We need antibiotics, too," I said simply, as blood trickled freely down my thigh.

The man sighed, inspecting both my leg and the lackluster bandage job we'd done on Ben's eye. "All right," he said finally. "I'm going to assume for now that you mean us no harm. But you're on your own with the damned cat."

He turned abruptly and went toward the back of the little pharmacy he'd stuffed us in. As heat radiated over my skin from the infection, I could only hope that he was finding me a pharmacist with some good drugs. The explorer moms hadn't been able to come up with penicillin.

I was adamant about Ben being treated first—but I sat down heavily in the middle of aisle three nonetheless, dizziness turning into a blinding white blocking my vision for a short moment. Ben was definitely my priority, but if the red lines reaching through my veins meant anything, I was in trouble.

Day Seven

Out of the Frying Pan, Into My Own Personal Hell

I hadn't told anyone about the infection, not even Ben. There wasn't much we could do about it, after all—and it wasn't like complaining about it would do me much good when Ben had an eye ripped out of his damned skull. Marley would only nag me and threaten to wash the wound out with the travel bottle of Scotch we'd discovered in one of the dad's cargo pockets. So I shut up and walked, just like the rest of the trudging injured.

Apparently that had been a stupid idea, as a pharmacist had found me our first day in Woodbury after I blanked out between Tampons and adult diapers. All of a sudden Marley had sat on my chest t hold me down and a bottle of iodine appeared out of nowhere—

Oh, holy hell no.

I screeched like a banshee as he began washing the crust off of the wound. "I told you! Ben first! Who even uses iodine anymore? What the hell is wrong with you?"

Marley glanced down at me. "While you were running away from the pharmacist into la-la land, the blue jeans guy—"

"Alex," the pharmacist grunted.

"Ahem. The blue jeans guy found the town doctor in whatever little corner of hell he normally resides in. Ben's in theoretically good hands; I looked at his degrees on the wall and they looked real, at least." She paused thoughtfully. "I guess they could have found the mortician and lied about his name to lull us into a false sense of security and—"

I shrieked again and twisted under her as the pharmacist did something unholy with my leg involving tweezers and the gauze that had stuck to the inside of the wound. Marley grabbed my hands and slammed them down onto the ground. "Would you shut up and hold still? He's trying to help. You're worse than Bacon," she muttered, then paled as reality caught up with her.

"I know," I whispered, closing my eyes briefly.

"I'm sorry. But all I can think about is the sound it made when she clawed me."

She softened, staring down at me for a long moment. "Well . . ." She swallowed audibly. "At least I shot Teddy in the head for trying to nail us. That bastard almost knocked the door down."

The pharmacist began to pull the somewhat mushy edges of infected skin together. My vision began to lighten and turn into that brilliant bright white again—I slid under the light until I no longer felt anything at all. I wanted to stay there forever.

I passed out, wishing with all my heart that I would wake up to a world where none of this had ever happened.

#

My thigh hadn't hurt quite this much even at the time of the attack. I tasted the bitterness of antibiotic pills that Marley must have shoved down my throat and frowned, struggling to sit up. I was back in aisle three. Ben was laying on the floor next to me, a pristine white bandage covering his not-an-eye.

I wanted nothing more than to talk to him, but I knew that he needed rest. I sighed, laying back down on the ugly beige linoleum, and wondered how exactly my life had come to this. One moment I was thinking about graduating and moving to Africa and the next, a freaking leopard decided I was a tea time meal and thankfully smacked me first rather than biting. It rushed me, all at once, to realize how damn lucky we were—that we hadn't been bitten and that it wasn't transmitted quite as easily as we'd feared. I knew that the likelihood of being infected by getting scratched—okay, zombie-infected, regular-infected was almost guaranteed—was slim, but with animals that weren't afraid of getting hurt, who knew what type of open wounds they'd have on their paws?

I shuddered, closing my eyes again. It was so close—so close, and I could have lost Ben. I could have lost Emma, who was growing increasingly close to my heart. Or Marley, who had been a friend before, and was a sister-in-arms now. We were so damn lucky to have each other that my heart grew the proverbial three sizes as I thought about it.

I heard voices toward the front of the pharmacy and frowned, peering underneath the shelves.

" . . . the north barricade. We think they're part of a group who split off from the ones the zoo people saw on their way here—half went to the zoo, the other half took the interstate and ended up here."

I heard blue jeans man's—Alex's—voice. He murmured inaudibly and I strained hard to hear. "Do we have enough ammo? Who's covering that wall?

What kind of weapons do we have that we can take over there?"

"Pistols, mostly. Private handguns that people kept in their damn nightstands. We'll never have enough ammo, but I think Mrs. Murray has a machete; she's probably already heading that way, screaming about kicking some zombie ass. That lady's seriously crazy."

"Great." Alex sighed heavily and I watched his boots pace back and forth. I frowned; this didn't sound like a man who pulled guns on people for no good reason. This sounded like a man who genuinely cared about his people; who was trying hard to make do with a situation that wasn't that great in the first place and was getting worse at every given moment. This sounded like . . . well, like a less-nuts version of Marley mixed with a little bit of Ben, really.

Ah, shit.

"I guess have the guys from Lumber Depot shore up the wall on that side, see what they can do to make it safer. Keep the kids away. If there's too many infected and it starts to look like they're coming over, shoot them. Do what you can."

I frowned, leaning back on my elbows. Two things were slowly becoming clear to me—we may have led the zombies, indirectly, to their camp by making a racket on our way here. And if that was true, it was our responsibility to do something about it. Secondly, these people weren't bad or dangerous; they were protecting their kids, making sure they had food and water and no zombies in their backyards. And that meant that we had a responsibility.

Crap. I slowly began to get to my feet.

"What are we going to do?" A female voice echoed from the front door.

"Not let them through," Alex replied softly. "I don't have a head count for what we've already lost, but I'm sure as hell not going to lose anyone or anything else on my watch if we can possibly help it."

"We don't have enough people for the three barricades we already have, and then there's the one that isn't even finished yet. What if they come from the East before we're done? Alex, this is too big for us. We need to find the government, the military—somebody has to be out there, somewhere. It's only been a week, somebody has to be helping people." She paused, and I heard her walking toward Alex. "Some of the people coming toward us aren't even infected. They're looters. How many of us can kill people that aren't infected?"

"We might have no choice. I'll cover the wall we haven't finished by myself if I have to. Just go, Amy. Help them round up the kids. We don't have time for this. Please."

I frowned, sitting back against the shelves, looking at Ben as he slept. They had normal, healthy people attacking their barricades? Looters—people who had been through this crap just the same as we had (minus some tigers) but instead of helping each other, had decided to grab crowbars and jack shit up. Anger rose fast as I stared at a box of Tampons. We had watched people die. I had watched *children* die. Ben lost an eye and Marley—Marley wouldn't tell anyone how badly she was truly injured. I could have lost my leg and that was probably still on the table, and we had people out there trying to hurt others that were just trying to survive?

Alex rolled up his sleeves and sighed lightly. He squared his shoulders, and I watched him through the shelves as he walked out the door. I sat in my aisle, frowning, when the pharmacist found me eavesdropping.

I held up my hands in innocence. "I have an idea," I said.

#

It was my turn to be the speech-maker. I had Marley round up the zoo denizens who'd wandered away, made offers to help, or generally caused a ruckus (that would be Emma and her friends) while I had been unconscious, and we wrangled them into the alley beside the pharmacy. It was surprisingly clean; no papers or bottles littered the ground, and no smell of human detritus penetrated the space. I wasn't sure what Woodbury did to their drunks and delinquents—maybe fed them chicken—but I was pretty impressed.

"So I think Woodbury is in trouble." Stating the obvious was a hobby of mine.

One of the parents—who seemed to have taken Hank as our de-facto leader and marched behind him the whole way from the zoo to Woodbury—snorted and spoke up. "You mean the guys who escorted us here at gunpoint and stuffed us in a pharmacy? They're in trouble? Cry me a river."

"We'll give them a couple of the kids' slingshots and call it good," another said. More tittering.

I closed my eyes, fingers rubbing at my clean bandage. I thought of Ben, finally able to rest with his eye bandaged properly, with real medication to soothe him. And I thought about Emma, who was growing up—albeit a little weirdly—in a normal life, until she was locked into our zoo. And I may have snapped a little.

"Cut the shit," I replied harshly. "They took us in and fixed our wounded; their children are playing with our children. It's *normal* here. There aren't zombie fucking *lions* here. And yeah, maybe they're a little overprotective of what they've got—but you would be too! If you had food and water and safe places to put these kids, wouldn't you be suspicious of people that were coming for you, especially if you had others trying to take it away?"

One of the mothers frowned. "Take it away?"

"There are looters," I replied heavily. "Like, legit looters that are coming to take the supplies that this town is using to keep things normal for their kids. Didn't Marley say they're even still running school here? I don't know how they've kept people from becoming infected. Maybe they're all vegetarians. Maybe they throw anyone who looks a little infected outside the walls. I don't know, they could be horrible people, but I really don't think they are. I think maybe we could have a chance here."

I could see the expressions on their faces changing from anger to confusion to a tiny amount of hope. We weren't so far gone that we'd forgotten what things were like—you know, electricity and civilization and Candy Crush. It had only been a week. But it had been the hardest week of our lives, and nobody wanted to repeat that in the Wild Blue Yonder if we could possibly avoid it. Someone who'd managed to power up the generators and keep their shit together seemed awfully good right about now.

"So . . . what's the plan?" Marley helped me along, asking the question I was trying to point everyone in the direction of.

"It's not like it's a hard plan or something," I said. "And it's not like there's a ton of details. But I heard blue jeans guy—his name is Alex—talking to one of his people, and it looks like they're pretty hard up on one of the exits out of the town. They've mostly got between houses shored up, and it's a pretty good ring around the center of town, but there's one exit they haven't gotten to yet, and there's a bunch of looters headed their way, and more zombies than that. And they've got shit for guns."

Emma squinted up at me, and I wondered how the hell she wasn't in bed by now. There was something seriously wrong with this kid. "You basically want us to go save the day, right?" Somewhere along the way, she'd found a machete, and I decided that I needed to have a serious talk with Ben about proper parenting.

Oh, shit. Parenting.

Minor life crisis aside, I nodded. "We all have weapons, and I think at this point we're either good with them or probably deserve to get eaten. It's been a rough couple of days," I acknowledged. "So we're going to head over to find Alex and keep that fucker alive until I can pay him back for putting a gun to Marley's head."

Marley cracked a smile. "That's my favorite part," she said. "Where do we start?"

#

I put Emma in charge of watching Ben. It was the only way I could think of to keep her out of the danger; she'd latched onto Ben pretty hard after the incident with the birds, and it wasn't hard to convince her to watch over him. I left the rest of the kids with her in the pharmacy and the pharmacist locked the door behind me. If the infected or the looters got through us, at least they wouldn't get to them.

Our ragtag band of zoo visitors and keepers—and one of the Channel 6 guys—gathered our weapons and started to head over to the south end of town. I heard it before I saw it—a desperate moaning, and something banging rhythmically against the metal barrier. This blockade wasn't as tall as the other ones; it reached from house to house, sure, but it barely rose up to cover Alex as he stood on top of a broken-down car with his rifle.

"There's no reason for any of this," he called down to who I presumed were looters. "We just let in some other folks from the zoo the other day; we'll help you, if we can."

All I could hear was the yelling, until the gunfire began.

Alex stood alone on top of a Ford Fiesta, sighting with his rifle and carefully aiming over the corrugated steel roofing panels that made up the start of a barricade. "That wasn't necessary," he replied mildly, to someone I couldn't see. "Also, I feel compelled to inform you that there are about forty infected persons heading this way behind you."

To Alex's credit, he did his best to be polite. He even issued a warning before the zombies got there. I did not, however, believe that he expected the molotov cocktail.

The rag burned against the dying light, flaring with the wind that battered our faces. I had a moment to be thankful that Ben wasn't there, and then the car lit on fire. It raced down the gas cap and a thin line of liquid below it, trickling like blood to the ground where the gasoline had leaked. Flames licked and flickered at the spilled gas, and heat rushed toward us. "Well, shit," Alex said, and jumped off the car.

We were just far enough not to feel the heat, but we could hear the pops of metal and the glass shattering. The car seemed to almost fold in on itself, rocking inward briefly then releasing its pressure.

Before long, it was all in flames. Meaning that the barrier was, effectively, down—and no one stood behind it. No one but us.

Sure enough, I saw plainly uninfected people staring at me from across the ruined barricade, holding up the same array of makeshift weapons that we had. Several did have guns, and I could only hope that we could hold the gap. It wasn't long before we would find out.

With a snarling yell, a man in a baseball cap ran forward, launching himself through the flames. More followed in quick succession, and over the flames, I could hear the moans.

Alex wasn't kidding when he'd warned the intruders.

I discovered how much better people-gauze was than vet gauze as I readied my stance. My leg actually felt somewhat solid; at least, not like a mushy mess. My time to think, however, ended rather abruptly as a man's wide smile filled my vision.

He could have been Mr. Freaking Rogers in the before, in his dress shirt and sweater, but now he was wielding a thick piece of wood as a baseball bat. He hefted it in his hands a few times, and I wondered what drove people to this; was it hunger? Fear? Or simple greed, that which had gotten us into this mess in the first place?

The surge of anger I felt as I blocked his bat with my axe answered me. “I don’t want to do this!” I yelled hoarsely. “What the hell is wrong with you?”

He smiled again, a kindly smile. “My kids all died,” he said simply. “So should you.”

I shrieked as I saw the bat cut the air towards my head and I swung blindly. A thick, meaty “chunk” accompanied the hit and my axe felt resistance, as if it was buried in a piece of wood.

It wasn’t.

My vision tunneled, narrowing down to a single frame—the sight of the man sliding off the axe that I’d buried in his chest. He fell to the ground in a heap, staring at me in surprise. I looked up briefly and saw equally dead eyes behind him. Those, at least, I could deal with.

I hefted the axe in my hands and flipped it blunt-side down, ignoring the gore washing down the handle, and swung hard enough to lose my balance. I slid in the blood of the man I’d killed, skidding on my heels and falling soundly in a disgusting mixture of blood and dirty water.

I hardly had a moment before I had to haul myself to my feet and land a solid blow to the side of the infected’s head. He went sideways, knocked away like a softball off a tee, and went silent.

If I thought about it for more than a moment, I'd fall apart.

The sound of the axe was all that I heard as I stood between Alex and Marley. Alex's gun went off next to me, and Marley was using her baseball bat decorated with thick, long nails pounded through it. I heard the meaty "thunk" noise again that meant I'd hit something.

I couldn't look to see if it was some*thing* or some*one*.

Sound came rushing back as I saw Alex rocking backward as if he'd been punched. Blood blossomed on the right shoulder of his green flannel shirt. He grimaced, holding his hand to the wound, and grabbed the pistol from his belt.

I screamed as a big stick swatted my thigh and hip, and I swung back, knocking over the woman who held the stick down with a blow to her chest. She stood up again quickly, and came at me again. And again.

I felt my arms stinging with fatigue and sweat rolled down into my eyes as I squared off with her. My thigh burned as if fire laced through it, penetrating my broken veins. I gasped raggedly, trying to breathe as I blocked her blows.

She wouldn't stop. There was a cold shiver in the

pit of my stomach as I realized that I had no choice. The zombie next to her was beginning to reach for me. I turned around my axe and buried it in her chest. It stuck while I pulled, finally yanking hard and stumbling backward. Alex caught me, his pistol digging into my lower back as he lightly pushed me up.

"Thanks," he hollered.

"Isn't that my line?"

He shot the zombie coming toward me with a single bullet.

"It is now," I added, looking around.

"You're saving our asses," he said grimly.

The world was unnaturally silent, suddenly. I could hear the soft patter of water falling to earth—until I looked over and realized it was blood. My chest heaved uncomfortably hard as I looked around and finally dropped my axe to the ground. I turned around to look at our motley group of defenders.

My bloody hands flew to my mouth as I surveyed the once-quiet, once-occupied street around me. Gore soaked into a woodpecker mailbox, thick globs of sticky pink tissue slowly dribbling to the ground below. A man had fallen on the sidewalk, hands outstretched toward the house he lay next to, never to get back up.

One of our explorer moms was being tourniqueted

by one of Alex's crew, her leg sitting three feet to her left. Another sat limply against the ruined barricade, and I could see shiny, white teeth through a gaping hole in his cheek.

I took a deep breath, and a head count—we were down six of us, five wounded, with the very late crew of Alex's picking up the zombie slack in our wake. Of the looters, I saw nothing but bodies.

I turned around again, sagging in shock and relief, when my eyes met Marley's.

"Oh, crap!"

Day Seven

Mourn Not the Undead

Marley was standing very still. I could almost see the thoughts flowing through her mind—what to do now, existential questions of destiny, fear. It was a look I was unaccustomed to seeing on her face; this was the girl who handled venomous snakes by herself and put it on YouTube. Fear was not something Marley knew an awful lot about.

Her hand curled protectively over her abdomen, where I'd seen her applying duct tape only a few days before. As her arm fell limply to her side, I saw that her original wound—a fearsome gash, at least an inch deep and maybe seven inches long—was nothing compared to this.

"Oh, God," I breathed, and rushed to catch her before she fell.

I ripped my shirt off and pressed it hard against her stomach, both to staunch the seeping blood and to force myself to believe that I hadn't seen what I saw. As I pushed down, I gagged, gasping as my hands felt something ropey and thick.

I'd seen her insides.

"You're gonna be fine," I told her firmly. You're going to be fine, and we can all find another zoo and build back up your venomous collection . . ."

Her hand fluttered to mine, resting gently over my fingers. "I don't think so, Lens," she said softly.

I looked into her eyes as my shirt soaked up her blood. "No," I replied, a sob escaping my mouth. "I refuse. How can I handle Ben without you? You're the voice of reason in my entire relationship. You're my adult-ier adult!"

A tear slowly collected dirt and blood as it slid down her cheek. "I've never been one for bullshit," she said, laughing weakly. "You can adult your own relationship. Treat him good, okay?" A soft gasp. "You sometimes suck with commitment."

She began to hiccup as she breathed, little stuttering inhalations. "Don't let me come back," she added.

"What?"

Marley grasped my wrist with surprising strength.

"You saw. Some of them die as people and come back. Don't . . . don't let me come back."

She gently pushed my hands away from her stomach. I could feel the blood filling the gaping chasm that was her abdomen. It spilled over the sides of her skin, puddling beside her.

"I won't," I whispered. "I promise."

"We won't," a husky voice added. "Though I don't know if I can forgive you for letting me sleep through the adventure you just had."

Marley's face lit up through her ashen pallor. "Ben. You missed the fun."

He sat down in the rapidly growing pool that sloshed against my hands as I attempted to shore up Marley's stomach with our hands, trying to dam the pool. He paused and shifted sheepishly so that his good eye faced her. "Still getting used to that," he murmured, to no one. He reached up and gently wiped away the tear she couldn't reach herself. "Did you get one for me?"

"Oh yeah," she breathed, voice hitching with every syllable.

The thick blood sat in its large lake between my hands, pushing against the shirt I'd held to her. The thin fabric slid to the ground, revealing the black pool of fluids that was only getting larger.

Ben picked up her limp hand and held it tightly in his.

"I pulled . . . some brains out with that last one," she hiccup-gasped again.

I smiled, tears running from beneath my eyelids and running down my face, cleansing the dirt and staining my soul. "Don't go," I said.

"I don't think I get a choice, Lens."

I sobbed, clutching her hand to my chest. It wasn't possible. She was my friend. She was my best friend. Best friends don't die.

"I'm not scared," she said, almost amused. "I always thought I'd die playing with snakes I shouldn't touch, though." She paused, inhaling sharply. The motion made the unsteady black lake spill over, exposing her muscles and intestines beneath.

"Too bad. Australia's got some real cool snakes," she exhaled, and her eyes slowly became like so much glass, reflecting the lights without a spark of their own.

"Fucking fuck!" I screamed, leaning down, beginning to sob against her chest. Ben held her hand and mine, sitting quietly with tears streaming down from his good eye. "It's not fair!"

Ben had no platitudes, no false words of comfort to placate me. "No, it isn't," he choked, staring down at her dolls' eyes "This new version of the world really sucks."

I clung to Marley's shirt, still not wearing my own, and hiccuped miserably. "I don't know what to do now," I whispered. "Not when she's not here to tell me."

Ben gathered me up in his arms and I lay my head against his chest, listening to the steady thump of his heartbeat. "We'll figure it out," he said. "Somehow. We'll find a way to make her proud."

It was then that Alex knelt down, still bleeding, but otherwise whole and hale. "You mourn," he said simply. "And you do better next time so that you never have to feel this way again. That's what you do." He smiled thinly with a crooked tilt to his mouth. "So far I apparently haven't done better next time quite well enough for the universe to treat me well."

As he walked away, Ben and I sat with Marley long after she grew cold. I felt my resolve slowly solidify and harden around my pain. I would do better. I would go back, perhaps, to save her snakes one day. I would maybe learn a new trade, become the world's first post apocalyptic snake handler. I would do better.

Most of all, I would *be* better. I'd be exactly what Marley had always told me I was: unstoppable.

#

It was difficult, making the slow trek back to the center of the city with our dead—true dead and twice-dead. Ben carried Marley's cold, lifeless form as I walked next to him, one slow step through the mud at a time.

The restaurant in the town square was the only place with enough space to lay our dead. We were few—three mothers, only one of whom had her children now; a lone father and his two sons; two explorer guides bewildered and baffled; and the near-dozen of presumably orphaned children left behind, guarded fiercely by Emma. They joined us at our impromptu wake. After we'd found all the bodies, Ben had quietly walked through the slightly haphazard rows and slid his knife behind the ear of each of our friends—and Alex did the same for his. My heart wrenched as I realized that this was our new world—one where corpses could stand again.

In the diner, there was silence. I could almost hear my own heart beating—breaking—as Ben and I stood next to Marley, bright red napkins serving as her funeral shroud. Alex was nowhere to be seen. The woman belonging to the voice I'd heard before in the pharmacy—Amy—stood behind the ancient cash register and cleared her throat.

"We've lost a lot," she began simply. "Friends, loved ones-and in some cases, probably our homes and former lives as well. I feel so stupid calling this the apocalypse, but when the dead begin to rise . . ." She cleared her throat, clearly uncomfortable. "We've had some radio contact with a few towns here and there, but the message seems to be the same—we're on our own. The combination of the flu and the tainted meat did some damage, but it was the dead rising that collapsed everything else. There's no military or government help. We're pretty sure they either don't even exist at this point or they're hiding somewhere in the mountains, avoiding the whole damn thing.

"All that to say . . . I can't think, I can't believe that our friends died in vain.

"Humanity has come together in the wake of this strange disaster. In the last week and a half, I've seen more neighbors helping neighbors, adults teaching children, and people who threw down over the casserole contest working side-by-side to get these barriers done."

Weak laughter. My hand strayed to Ben's, holding his fingertips lightly.

"We don't know how bad it is—but we can guess. We don't know how widespread it is—but the last newscast we saw showed a plane down over the Pacific. This was our first week of a new world."

She paused, surveying the tables in front of her. "It wasn't a good week," someone murmured softly.

Amy nodded and straightened. "No, it wasn't a good week, and it'll get worse before it gets better. But I think we owe it to our faithful friends who passed to make sure that it DOES get better. I think that's the only legacy any of us can hope for."

She sat down slowly, and a heavyset man with a bloody baseball cap and a dirty apron stood and squinted at us. "If you're able, we need some help in the football field before the service. Any volunteers will be welcome. Thank you."

"What's in the football field?" someone asked.

Ben and I glanced at each other. The man had the grace to look proud, rather than embarrassed. "It's the only place with enough land for the size graveyard we're going to need."

One man stood, and then another. I closed my eyes briefly as I realized that Marley would have been the first one out there with a shovel in hand and a friendly word. The frank permanence of death was astounding, and it built a wall in my brain that I couldn't walk around. I would have to walk into it, over and over again, until Marley's death became a sad memory instead of a physical blow. I lay my hand on Ben's arm as he made to stand.

"You need rest," I murmured.

"So do you," he shot back, but settled in his chair. "At least I was respectfully in a drug-induced nightmare while you were out slaying zombies on a bum leg."

It occurred to me that we may have, so simply, found our new places in the apocalypse. As much as he didn't want to admit it, Ben's depth perception (or lack thereof) was now verging on "liability." I knew he'd find his equilibrium as time wound on, but for now, I had to protect the both of us.

And Emma.

And the half-feral pack of orphaned explorer kids that needed someone, anyone to care.

I sighed and almost laughed as I realized I'd carried my axe with me to the "wake." Already, it was setting in. No more time to play video games and eat six packs of Ramen in one night—this time, I *was* the adultier adult.

Ah, crap.

#

The day dawned sunny and crisp, the last vestiges of leaves falling gently on newly turned earth. I watched as a red maple leaf drifted over the football field and landed on the edge of a grave adjacent to Marley's. Unbeknownst to us, the kids had spent the night and into the small hours of the morning using an axe Emma had "found" to destroy the half-door to the pharmacy counter, and carefully hacked it into a grave marker for their hero, Marley. I assumed that Emma had vandalized a craft or hobby store for the rather impressive-quality paints, and I fervently hoped she hadn't been the one carving with the X-acto knife.

Marley would ever remain their hero for getting them out of the zoo. If only the rest of us could have such a legacy.

What they didn't know about taxonomy, they made up for with color and attention to detail. The snakes they'd painted may have had only the barest resemblance of what Marley had shown them, but a beautiful wreath of writhing snakes hung around her carefully engraved name. They didn't know her surname, but her epitaph spoke volumes:

Marley
Savior and Snake Friend
Lost in the Rising of the Dead
Godspeed.

It was rather poetic for a group of teens and pre-teens, and I smiled. The uprising. That wasn't a phrase I'd thought to attach to the disaster before, but it fit, somehow. The rising of our nightmares into true terrors. The kids seemed to be adapting to post-zombie—well, current-zombie, really—life much easier than the rest of us. While we spent our time shoring up defenses and sobbing to each other over the flickering electricity and the lack of food deliveries to the grocery store, they had formed their semi-feral pack of children with their own society of rules and leaders fairly quickly.

As Emma slipped her small, but sturdy hand into mine, I marveled at how this child—still with broken bones!—had shot to the top of the pack. Her fierceness gave me hope that while the rest of us tried to reclaim our humanity and keep it safe, Emma and her tribe would never lose theirs. It had only changed.

Money no longer meant status. Charisma was everything. I needed to take a few lessons from Emma before dealing any more with Alex.

The sun crested the top of the stadium and I could see my breath in the air. Alex stood with Amy at the head of the arena, staring across the field at the 20-or-so graves neatly lined by the endzone. I had a feeling it wouldn't be the last time we met here, consigning our dead unto the earth.

The undead wouldn't stop—they didn't know how to. They were an unending stream of hunger and the desire to infect us all. We were one of the last bastions of defense—a pocket of humanity in the wake of disaster, hopefully the smallest and not the last. As Alex began to speak, I stood quietly beside Marley's carefully bed sheet-wrapped form, staring at the sifted earth beside her. His words twisted and whirled around me and I hung on to the barest fragments of phrases, unable to look away from the somewhat large graveyard that had sprung up overnight.

Each grave had a bed sheet-wrapped denizen; I briefly wondered if anyone had any linens left. Two adults and often a child or two stood next to each grave, waiting.

The sun finally popped over the stadium almost audibly as it arose in one swift breath. Alex exhaled and nodded, and we gathered up the sheets. Woodbury didn't have a backhoe in town limits. We were on our own.

Emma stood at the head of Marley's grave, holding hard onto the wooden tombstone as Ben, myself, and one of Woodbury's women helped us to gently lower Marley into the hole. It was lined gently with pine needles, and my heart lurched at the unseen kindness.

Marley lay entwined in that clean, white sheet. Ben had spent all night with his head tilted to one side, sewing her skin closed for the sake of modesty. Emma had cast about the town, forcing every child to look through their toy boxes until she found it. She leaned as far as she could toward Marley and gently deposited a wooden, movable snake onto her chest.

"There," she said, breathing heavily as she stood. "Now she won't be alone."

She stared down at the snake for one breath, maybe two, and collapsed at Ben's feet with a stifled sob.

He crouched and gathered her against his chest as I stood guard over Marley, awaiting the men with shovels. He held her quietly, letting her cry without shame; they sat at the graveside and mourned together, and there was something beautiful, something purely human in that embrace. I closed my eyes and took my own moment to breathe, looking down at Marley one last time.

I fished a key from my pocket.

Ben frowned, trying to shift for a better vantage point to see what I was doing. "What's that?"

"I'm not sure your apartment is still there, and based on the videos I saw, I'm pretty sure we don't want to go back into the city, either." I sat with Ben and Emma for a long time, staring down at Marley. "So I guess this is my way of resuming our previous conversation. Do you want to stay here? Do you still want me to move in with you?"

"You're discussing this at a funeral?"

I looked down at the dirt being gently lowered onto the shroud and tried to smile. Emma sucked her thumb quietly as she lay her head on Ben's lap. "I'm pretty sure Marley would've been the first person to tell me it was about damn time."

Emma looked at us out of the corner of her eye, then dropped her gaze.

"She'd also be the first to tell you to stop looking at me like that," I added quietly, glancing down at Emma with a smile.

"Like what?" Her voice was muffled by Ben's jacket.

"Like you don't know that you're coming with us," Ben said simply. "I need my fierce protector with me until I learn how to protect myself again."

She frowned carefully, peeking up at us.

"Coy doesn't suit you," I said. "You're family now. All that's left is to pick a house nobody died in and help Alex rebuild the fences and burn all the chicken we see."

"I never want to see another chicken nugget again," she breathed, and wrapped her arms around my waist.

We watched the dirt begin to fill the grave. It

marked the line between Before and After. Before, my Quagga project. After, seed germination and growing crops, if the world truly was in such a wrecked state. Before, academia and video games. After, a post-apocalyptic nut who would have to rely on Young Adult books to prepare her for a country with no leadership, no cure, and people trying to eat us.

As the sun began to rise in earnest, people stood and dusted themselves off, checking in with Alex and leaving for the haphazard work detail he'd created. I pulled Ben and Emma to their feet.

"I'm going to help Alex fix this cluster," I said finally. "Organizational skills don't seem to be his forte. I overheard the school lunch lady saying she was on board-sawing duty."

"What are we doing?" Emma, of course, took charge.

"You are finding Amy and getting us somewhere to stay," I said.

She paused. "I think Marley would like that," she said simply. She and Ben walked away to find Amy, hand-in-hand, Emma gently leading Ben as best as she could.

I sat quietly by the grave long into the morning, far past the time the rest of the graves were filled, and only stirred when I heard unfamiliar voices shouting. It was a healthy sound, one of construction and cohesiveness, a common goal. I smiled, standing, and turned into the wind. I was beginning to feel like we'd maybe be okay here. The explorers could settle down and start cataloging nature and plants for us; we could all heal from the oozing mass of our losses. We could form a party to go out and find out how widespread this really was.

The breeze brought with it the smell of the last leaves of autumn, the copper taste of blood and the promise that winter was coming. As I turned to leave the graveyard, I frowned, straining my ears. I heard a noise that sounded strangely like a leopard that I'd met before.

Oh, crap.

www.ingramcontent.com/pod-product-compliance
Lightning Source LLC
LaVergne TN
LVHW091110080826
845145LV00008B/1869